The Silence After

By: Britt Wolfe

This Novella Is Dedicated to:

The truth tellers.

This is for everyone who has stood with nothing but their own voice as armour, speaking what is right even when the world tried to drown them out. For those who chose integrity over comfort, who carried the weight of honesty while others built their lives on lies.

This is for the ones who were punished for refusing to look away, who were called liars, troublemakers, or worse, simply because they would not bend to silence. For those who bore the cost of telling the truth and still chose it anyway.

And this is for those still standing. For the ones who know that doing the right thing is rarely the easy thing, and that courage is often a quiet, relentless persistence. For those who live their lives not for applause, but because their hearts know the difference between what is easy and what is good.

I know the ache of it. I know the loneliness of holding the line when the crowd turns against you. But I also know this—there is strength in truth, even when it shatters. There is dignity in refusing to betray yourself.

You are not alone. You are not foolish. You are proof that integrity matters, even when the cost is everything.

This story is for you.

The Silence After
Is Inspired by: *Cassandra*
by Taylor Swift

Since the moment I first heard *Cassandra*, I was struck by the rawness in its bones—this wasn't just a retelling of an old myth, it was a mirror. It's a song about what it costs to tell the truth, about the fury unleashed when you dare to speak against power, and the unbearable quiet that follows when the truth finally comes to light. Beneath its fury lies a hollowing ache —the loneliness of knowing you were right, but that no one cared enough to listen until it was too late.

For me, Cassandra became more than a song. It became a reflection of what it means to live with integrity in a world that often punishes you for it. In family dynamics, in cycles of silence, in the way cruelty masquerades as care—there are echoes of Cassandra everywhere. This novella plants the emotions of that song into the life of a girl who grows up voiceless, who learns too early that truth can be both a weapon and a wound, and who discovers the devastating reality that being right does not always mean being heard.

This is a story about survival, about the unbearable weight of carrying what others refuse to see. It's about a daughter who tried to tell her story, who reached for justice again and again, and who was met not with vindication but with silence. Yet it's also about strength—about the courage it takes to keep standing when the crowd turns against you, and the quiet dignity of living in alignment with what is good and true, even when it costs you everything.

I hope this story resonates with you the way Cassandra has with me—an ode to truth-tellers, to resilience, and to the ones who keep going, even when the truth comes out and all it is, is quiet.

Peace, Love, and Inspiration,

Britt Wolfe

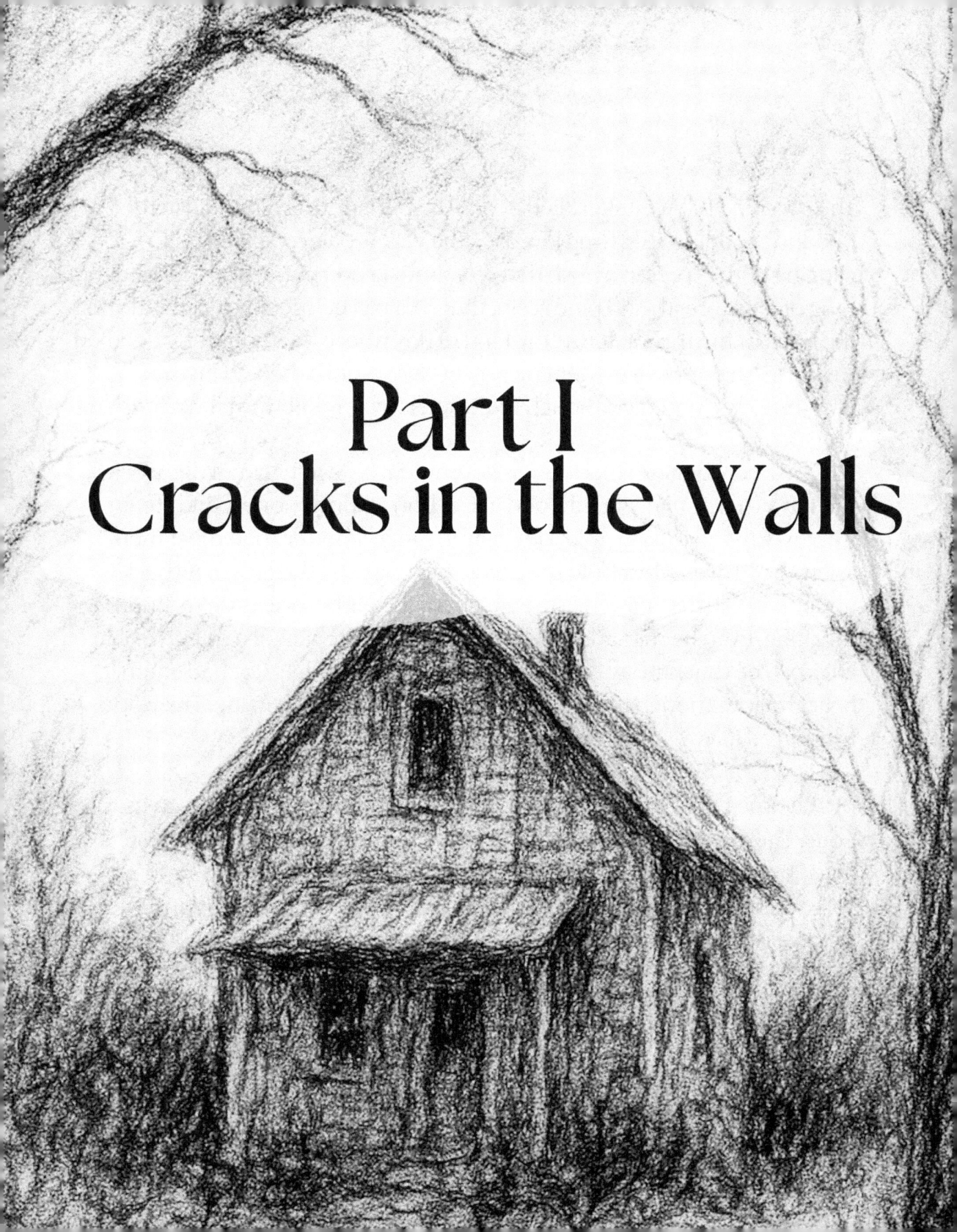

Part I
Cracks in the Walls

The Day the Lights Went Out
Then

The morning Bill Whitaker died began as so many mornings did in the Pocono foothills: a fog lying low over the valley, pale as spilled milk, clinging to the trees in a hush that felt almost reverent. The air carried the tang of damp earth and pine resin, that sharp green scent that could sting the back of the throat. It was the kind of day where the mountains seemed to fold in on themselves, holding secrets close, and where even the birdsong was muted, as though the woods already knew what was coming.

Bill had been logging since he was seventeen. It wasn't glamorous work, but it was honest and steady, and in Carbon County, honest and steady were worth more than gold. He knew the forest better than most men knew their wives—he could tell a tree's strength by the give of its bark under his palm, could sense the weight of the air before a storm. But that morning, even he missed what lurked beneath the skin of a massive black cherry tree that had stood for decades along the ridge. Rot had eaten its heart hollow, though the trunk looked solid from the outside. The wood whispered its weakness only to itself.

By the time Bill's chainsaw bit into it, the decay had already chosen its hour. The cut was clean, his stance practiced, his breath even. He had felled hundreds of trees like it. But the trunk betrayed him in a sudden, splintering sigh—an echo that cracked across the ridge like a gunshot. The tree twisted as it fell, its weight no longer predictable, and before Bill could move, before the shout of his co-worker could even fully leave the man's mouth, the trunk split, shuddered, and crashed sideways.

The force drove him to the earth with a sound more bone than wood. It was over before his eyes had time to register surprise.

By noon, word spread through Jim Thorpe the way word always did—through the clatter of the diner, through the slow crawl of pickup trucks past one another, windows rolled down, voices low. *Bill Whitaker's gone. Freak accident. A good man, taken young.*

Abby sat on the porch with their newborn daughter tucked against her chest, the baby's head no heavier than a fist. Her son, Darryl, ten years old and already carrying himself like a man, leaned against the railing, watching the line of cars pull up to their small house on the edge of town. His face was pale, but his jaw was set in that Whitaker way, stubborn and tight, as though clenching hard enough might stop the world from shifting beneath his feet.

Inside, the kitchen counter groaned under the weight of casseroles. Funeral food: lasagnas, green bean bakes, ham loaves wrapped in foil. Each dish bore the silent hope that starch and fat could do the impossible —fill the hole where a husband and father had been. Women from church clucked and whispered, their perfume mingling with the smell of creamed soup and scorched coffee. They carried on in hushed tones, careful not to let the children hear the pity in their voices.

But pity carried. It slipped under doors, wove itself through walls, settled into the corners of a house until it was all that lived there.

Abby smoked one cigarette after another, her hands trembling just enough to betray her composure. She was thirty-four, with dark hair always falling loose from its pins, skin freckled from summers that felt like another lifetime. She hadn't asked for condolences, hadn't asked for neighbours on her porch or for casseroles filling her fridge. She wanted quiet. Instead, the house breathed with other people's grief, suffocating her own.

When the funeral came, the town turned out in its Sunday best. St. Mark's Lutheran Church filled with familiar faces, bowed heads, and the faint rustle of tissues pulled from coat pockets. The coffin was simple oak, polished until it gleamed like honey. Abby stood at the front with Cassandra in her arms, too dazed to weep, while Darryl shifted from one foot to the other, his tie crooked, his hair combed so flat it looked plastered.

The pastor spoke of Bill as a man of steady faith and steady hands, a man who provided, who loved the land, who never shirked his duty. Abby stood stiff beside the coffin, a child at her breast, another at her side, listening as the town turned her husband into something larger than life. But she had known him in the quiet hours: his laugh, his temper when the bills stacked too high, the way he rubbed his shoulder when the ache set in. She had loved him, yes, but she had also counted on him. And now that certainty— steady as the ground under her feet—had cracked, leaving her swaying, untethered.

At the graveside, the November wind cut sharp through coats. Dirt hit wood with a hollow thud, final in its simplicity. Darryl flinched at the sound. Abby lit another cigarette before the first handful of earth had even been thrown, her free hand tightening around the bundle of Cassandra's blankets as though anchoring herself to the only proof that life continued.

For Cassandra, memory would never reach this day. She would grow up with the story instead—the way people told it, the way they shaped it into something she was expected to carry. A father lost before she could know him, a tragedy she was too young to remember but old enough to feel etched into the walls of her home.

In the weeks that followed, the house filled with silence that wasn't silence at all. It was the silence of absence—the missing slam of Bill's boots by the door, the missing whistle he carried from the woods, the missing hum of his voice low in the kitchen at dawn. Abby filled it with smoke and bitterness. Darryl filled it with resentment he didn't have the words for. Cassandra filled it, unknowingly, with the breath of a baby who would grow into that silence as though it were air.

The casseroles cooled. The neighbours stopped knocking. Winter set in, a heavy grey drape across the town. The Whitaker house sagged inward, a small structure on a small street, the kind of house that remembered every word spoken within it.

And Cassandra, though too young to know it, was already learning her first truth: that sometimes the light goes out before you ever see it, and you are left to stumble in the dark with only other people's stories to tell you what it once looked like.

Winter thickened in Carbon County, coating the ridges in frost, filling the hollows with a damp that clung to clothes and hair. The Whitaker house seemed to absorb it, the walls exhaling chill no matter how hot the radiators hissed. Abby sat most evenings at the kitchen table, chain-smoking with an ashtray already full, the baby monitor hissing beside her like a static ghost.

Darryl began to walk differently, shoulders hunched as if he carried more than his ten years. He took to watching the men at the barbershop after school, memorizing how they stood with their hands in their pockets, how they spat opinions like bullets. He had no patience for the pity that drifted his way in whispers. When the teachers gave him that soft-eyed look, he bristled. When neighbours brought casseroles in December, he refused to eat them, pushing the fork around his plate as though the food itself were an insult.

At night, when Abby closed herself in her room and the baby finally slept, Darryl would sometimes creep into the living room and sit in Bill's chair. The worn recliner still smelled faintly of sawdust and sweat, though the scent was fading. He would grip the arms of the chair until his knuckles whitened, daring the world to tell him he wasn't the man of the house now.

But he wasn't his father. He was only a boy learning early that grief curdles if left too long unattended.

The town, too, moved on. That was the way of small places: tragedy struck hard but not forever. A new baby was born, a wedding was announced, someone's truck slid into a ditch, and the focus shifted. Bill's absence lingered in Abby's house, but not at the hardware store, not at the mill, not even at St. Mark's, where his name was spoken less each Sunday.

Cassandra would never know her father's voice, though neighbours liked to tell her he had sung low and steady when he worked, a hum that kept rhythm better than any metronome. She would never know the feel of his hand steadying her first steps, never know the weight of his approval. Instead, she would know him only through the fragments people left behind: "He was a good man." "Never missed a day's work." "Loved that boy of his." Words pressed into her like labels, stories she was supposed to believe without ever having lived them.

And Abby—oh, Abby—grief didn't soften her. It sharpened her edges. She cursed more. She snapped quicker. She began to speak of life as though it had conspired against her, as though Bill's death was not chance but proof of a cosmic cruelty that singled her out. Cigarette smoke stained the curtains, beer cans collected by the back step, and bitterness became her only constant companion.

She carried Cassandra like a burden, not a gift. The baby cried; Abby hissed at her to hush. The baby smiled; Abby turned away. She saw in Cassandra's face not hope but the last thing Bill had left her to care for, and it tasted like punishment.

On the porch one evening, as snow began to fall, Abby exhaled smoke into the cold air and muttered to a neighbour, "That girl cost me my husband. If I hadn't been home with her, maybe I'd have been there, maybe I'd have stopped him."

The neighbour winced, half-glancing at the bundled baby in Abby's arms, but said nothing. In small towns, silence was its own complicity.

Darryl heard. He stood in the doorway, fists clenched, and felt something knot inside him that would never quite come undone.

The funeral had been nothing in Cassandra's unformed memory, but for Darryl it stayed sharp. He remembered the sound of dirt on wood, the cough of the pastor when his throat caught, the way his mother's hand trembled on her cigarette as though she might shatter. He remembered the casseroles and the whispers, the sense that everyone was watching to see how the Whitakers would collapse. And he remembered swearing, quietly to himself, that he wouldn't.

But strength, in Darryl's young hands, hardened into cruelty. When the world gave him no gentleness, he decided to mirror it.

The Whitaker home became a place where grief wasn't spoken, only performed in sharp words and slammed doors. The baby grew in the cradle of that silence, absorbing it into her bones. Cassandra would never know the sound of her father's chainsaw, never hear the rhythm of his boots on the porch. Instead, she would know the click of her mother's lighter, the scrape of her brother's anger, the chill that settled into every room like a cold winter.

And though she was too young to name it, she would learn this truth early: that a house can mourn long after the people inside it have stopped.

The Whitaker house wore its grief like mildew—something that crept into the walls and clung to every surface, staining what could not be scrubbed clean. From the outside, it looked ordinary enough: a squat frame of weather-beaten siding, its paint once white but now closer to the colour of ancient bones, roof patched with shingles that never quite matched. But inside, the air carried a heaviness that pressed on the lungs, a sour blend of cigarette smoke, beer, and damp wood that had absorbed too many winters.

Abby filled the space like a storm cloud. She moved through the rooms with the restlessness of someone who could never quite settle, her lighter snapping open and shut in rhythm with her breath. The ashtrays overflowed no matter how often Darryl emptied them, the kitchen counters littered with pill bottles whose labels blurred with grease and dust. Some were legitimate—prescribed for nerves or sleep—but others came from friends, neighbours, a cousin with connections. Pills to wake her up, pills to calm her down, pills to turn down the volume of a life she hadn't asked to live.

She was unpredictable, her moods swinging like a screen door in the wind. One moment, she would sit at the kitchen table humming tunelessly, her hand stroking Cassandra's hair almost tenderly. The next, her palm would crack against Cassandra's cheek for spilling milk, for crying too loudly, for nothing at all. Abby's hand left more than one bruise that Cassandra learned to cover by tugging her sleeves lower, by lowering her eyes when the school nurse looked too long.

Darryl watched and learned. At ten, he was already tall for his age, all elbows and defiance. He saw his mother's cruelty not as shame but as survival. If the world was going to take what you loved without warning, better to be the taker than the taken. He parroted her words, her tones, testing out meanness the way other boys tested out baseball gloves. When Abby sneered, he sneered harder. When Abby shouted, he raised his voice louder. He discovered early the satisfaction of seeing Cassandra flinch.

For Cassandra, life in the Whitaker house became a series of strategies, a daily ritual of avoiding landmines. She was small, quiet, birdlike in her movements, her brown eyes always searching for cues. She learned the texture of her mother's footsteps, the difference between the heavy, stumbling tread of liquor and the quick, sharp taps of anger. She learned to bring her mother cigarettes before being asked, to fetch Darryl a soda from the fridge before he could demand. She lived on the edge of anticipation, convinced that perfection might be a kind of shield.

But perfection is fragile, and Cassandra was a child. A spilled cup, a misplaced toy, a laugh too loud, and the storm would break again.

At night, when the house was dark except for the ember of Abby's last cigarette glowing in the ashtray, Cassandra sometimes crept to the window. From her small room at the back of the house, she could see the slope of the mountains in the distance, black against the moonlight. She imagined that beyond those ridges, life must be softer, quieter. She wrote stories in her head—about girls who ran into the woods and found doorways into better worlds, about families who kept their promises, about homes that didn't feel like cages.

The Whitaker house itself seemed to conspire against her. The wallpaper peeled at the seams, revealing plaster scarred by years of damp. The carpet smelled faintly of mould no matter how often Abby doused it in carpet powder. Every window stuck in its frame, glass fogged with age. Even the air had weight, as though grief had settled into the beams when Bill died and refused to leave. Cassandra felt it pressing down on her chest when she tried to sleep, a heaviness that whispered she would never escape.

She carried that heaviness to school, where teachers saw only a quiet girl with hollow cheeks and a tendency to flinch. Friends were scarce; what mother wanted her child spending time in the Whitaker house? Still, Cassandra tried. She drew pictures for her mother, folded laundry, scrubbed dishes until her fingers wrinkled. Once, she baked a cake from a recipe in the back of a magazine, its lopsided frosting slathered with hope. Abby took one bite, declared it dry, and dumped the rest into the trash.

"Stop wasting time," she muttered, lighting another cigarette. "You'll never be anything."

The words sank into Cassandra deeper than any bruise.

Darryl, fed by their mother's disdain, learned to turn it into games only he found amusing. He mocked her voice, his laughter like shards. At dinner he nudged and needled, flicking Cassandra's ears, telling her she was stupid, worthless, nothing. But at night the cruelty changed shape. He would slip beneath her covers, breath sour with secrets, whispering words meant to pin her in place. Cassandra lay stiff as stone, her stillness the only shield she had. It was never enough to protect her.

And Abby did nothing. Sometimes, she even smirked, proud of the hardness she saw blooming in her son.

Cassandra learned to disappear into corners, into notebooks, into silence. Her attempts at pleasing them never held. No amount of tidying, no careful words, no perfect grades could pierce the armour of Abby's bitterness or Darryl's cruelty. She lived as a ghost in her own house, haunting the rooms of her childhood, carrying her father's absence like a second skin, though she had never met the man.

Yet even ghosts can dream. And in the quietest hours, when her mother's snores shook the walls and Darryl left her bed for his own, Cassandra held a flashlight beneath her blanket and scribbled in a cheap spiral notebook. She wrote about the forest, about girls with secrets, about monsters that looked an awful lot like family. She wrote herself doorways, wrote herself windows, wrote herself wings. Her words smelled faintly of mildew from the house, of ink and desperation, of a child trying to save herself with stories.

The Whitaker house would stand for decades more, sagging deeper into itself, but even then Cassandra knew—it would never feel like home. It would only ever feel like the place she had to survive long enough to leave.

The Betrayal

To Cassandra, the house seemed to breathe differently when Darryl was home. It was subtle—shadows stretched longer, the air grew heavier, as if the walls themselves tensed in anticipation. Cassandra felt it in her stomach before her mind caught up, a twisting knot that made her hands clammy and her throat tight.

Darryl was taller now, his limbs stretched into awkward angles, his voice cracking into manhood. He strutted through the house with a new authority, as though he had inherited not just their father's boots but his right to command. Abby encouraged it, calling him her man, leaning on him to carry groceries, to fetch her cigarettes, to shout down the bill collectors when they called. He liked it. It gave him a power he had never earned, a power he turned against the only person smaller than him.

The night Cassandra realized she had reached the end of what she could endure, the house was hushed except for the groan of floorboards and the low hum of the refrigerator. Abby had passed out in her room, a pill bottle tipped beside the ashtray, the stale smoke of her presence lingering in the hall.

Cassandra sat cross-legged on her bed, a notebook balanced on her knees. She wrote by the weak beam of a dying flashlight, words tumbling in crooked lines about a cat who had turned into a werepanther and was terrorizing the neighbourhood.

The door creaked open. Darryl filled the frame, his face half-shadow, half-smirk. He didn't speak—just watched. Cassandra froze, the pencil trembling in her hand. When he finally stepped into the room, the air seemed to shrink, pulling tight.

He usually came when she was asleep, leaving her to wake uncertain if it had been a dream. But this time she was awake, wide-eyed, no shield of disbelief to soften the edges. This time was different.

What happened next lived in her body more than her memory. The sequence dissolved; the movements scattered. What remained was the violence of it, sharp and merciless. She remembered the weight of his presence pressing her into the mattress, the confusion of laughter turned cruel, the way her breath caught on fear's sharp edge. She remembered the walls leaning closer, the wallpaper's curling edges like teeth. She remembered wishing the floor would split open and swallow her whole.

Afterward, she lay rigid, staring at the ceiling, the smell of mildew and smoke pressing down like another blanket. Tears slipped silent into her hair. Darryl left as though nothing had happened, the creak of the closing door almost gentle, a parody of tenderness.

But this time she couldn't tell herself it had been imagined. This time her body bore the evidence—bruises in the shape of fingers, bite marks sharp as accusations, pain that lived in every step.

For days she carried it like a shard of glass beneath her ribs. She tried to write it out, filling pages with jagged words, but each line only cut deeper. At last, unable to hold it alone, she carried the wound to her mother.

Abby was in the kitchen, cigarette smoke coiling into the air, a glass of something amber sweating on the table. Cassandra stood in the doorway, clutching the hem of her shirt, her voice trembling as she spoke. She didn't have the language for it—no child ever does. What came out was broken, halting, half-sentences and stammered truths.

Abby stared at her for a long moment, then exhaled smoke through her nose. "What the hell are you talking about?"

"I—I don't like when Darryl—" Cassandra began, but Abby cut her off with a sharp gesture.

"You stop right there. You don't come into my kitchen and spread lies about your brother."

Cassandra shook her head, desperate. "I'm not lying. He—"

Abby rose to her feet, chair scraping against linoleum.

She stormed up the stairs and into Darryl's room. Cassandra followed, her heart hammering, hope flickering that maybe—just maybe—her mother would stop what was happening to her.

Darryl sat up in bed, eyes wide at the intrusion. Abby's voice cracked like a whip. "She's in there telling me you touched her. You tell me right now, did you?"

The room was silent for a beat. Then Darryl's face hardened. "What? No. God, Mom, no. She's making shit up again. She's crazy."

Cassandra's mouth opened, but no sound came. The look Abby turned on her was worse than any slap.

"You lying little bitch," Abby hissed, advancing on her. "How dare you? After everything he's been through, after what this family's lost—you're gonna drag your brother's name through the mud?"

The slap came swift, the sting blooming hot across Cassandra's cheek. She stumbled, the taste of copper flooding her mouth.

"Don't you ever say something like that again," Abby spat. "Not to me, not to anyone. You hear me?"

Darryl watched from his bed, a smirk tugging at the corner of his mouth.

Cassandra nodded, tears burning her eyes, though she tried to hold them back. Crying only made it worse.

That night, she lay in bed with the covers pulled to her chin, her cheek still throbbing, her chest aching with a truth she had tried to give voice to only to have it shoved back down her throat. She learned something unshakable in that moment: truth did not matter. Not here. Not in this house. People believed what they wanted to believe, and Abby wanted a son she could protect, not a daughter she could defend.

And just as the injustice of it began to settle, hardening into a kind of bleak acceptance, the door creaked open. Cassandra lay still, listening to the sound of Darryl's footsteps padding across the floor. He snickered softly as he slid beneath her covers.

From then on, Cassandra's silence was not just survival—it was necessity. She wrote more furiously, scribbling until her fingers cramped, but she never spoke of Darryl again. Not to her mother, not to teachers, not to anyone. The truth, she understood, was a luxury reserved for people whose voices mattered.

Hers did not

The entire house almost seemed to sigh with relief at her silence, settling deeper into its rot, content to keep its secrets. Cassandra carried them like weights, pressing her small body into corners, into notebooks, into dreams of escape.

But the lesson remained, carved into her like scripture: truth could be told, but it would not be heard.

And in that silence, Darryl, and the evil of him, thrived.

Shadows in the Mirror

By the time Cassandra was thirteen, the Whitaker house had long ago stopped feeling like a place she lived in and started feeling like a place she endured. Its walls leaned closer every year, their stains darkening, the wallpaper curling like parchment ready to burn. The mirrors, speckled with age, reflected back a girl she barely recognized—hollow eyes, lips pressed tight as if holding in words too dangerous to speak. She would stare at herself until her vision blurred, trying to see the version of her she carried in her head: the one who wasn't afraid, the one who might survive this place. But the reflection never changed.

Depression crept in not like a sudden storm but like a slow flood, rising inch by inch until she was drowning in it. She woke each morning with a weight on her chest that pressed her deeper into the mattress. At school, she drifted through classes like a ghost, her hand sometimes shooting up with the right answer, only to drop when she remembered that being noticed came with consequences. She spoke less, wrote more. Her notebooks filled with crooked lines that looked more like maps than homework—routes she wished she could follow out of her life.

She discovered pain was one thing she could control. A razor blade, sharp and discreet, tucked into the back corner of her sock drawer beneath balled-up cotton and mismatched pairs. She didn't use it every day, but knowing it was there was its own kind of comfort, a door she could open when the walls pressed too tightly. The sting of it was brief, clean, real—so much simpler than the sprawling mess of her mother's rage or her brother's smirk. The small lines she carved into her skin were secret, hidden beneath long sleeves, their existence a language spoken only to herself.

The library became her sanctuary. Not the one at school, always buzzing with whispers and eyes that followed her, but the Jim Thorpe Public Library, housed in the old stone building with its heavy oak doors and ceilings that smelled faintly of dust and varnish. The librarians knew her by name but never asked questions. They let her sit for hours in the far corner, knees tucked under her, notebooks spread across the table. Here, she breathed easier. Here, no one called her crazy or liar or nothing. Here, she could invent worlds.

She filled spiral notebooks with horror stories. Monsters crept out of basements that spoke suspiciously like her own. Ghosts haunted children in houses with siding that sagged in the same places as the Whitakers'. Her villains often wore familiar faces—though disguised with sharper teeth, with claws, with the kind of obvious evil no one could deny. In her stories, the children always saw the truth. In her stories, they were believed.

At night, she wrote by flashlight, the same way she had as a child, the pencil moving so fast the lead snapped and smudged. She wrote until her hand cramped, until the fear in her chest loosened just enough to let her sleep. The notebooks piled under her bed like bricks, a foundation of words she built when everything else around her was crumbling.

Abby noticed, of course. She noticed everything when it suited her.

"Always scribbling lies," she muttered one afternoon, plucking a notebook off the kitchen table where Cassandra had left it while washing dishes. She flipped through the pages, her fingers smudged with graphite. "What kind of garbage is this?"

Cassandra's heart pounded in her ears. "Just stories," she whispered.

"Stories." Abby barked a laugh and tossed the notebook onto the counter. "You think you're some kind of writer? Newsflash—you ain't. You're nothing. Just like your daddy, breaking his back for nothing. At least he worked. You sit there with your head in the clouds, making up nonsense nobody wants to hear."

The words burned more than any slap ever did. Stories were the one place Cassandra felt whole, the one place she could shape the world instead of being crushed by it. Abby's ridicule cut through that sanctuary like a knife.

Still, Cassandra kept writing. She wrote in smaller, tighter script, hunched over her notebook in her room, ears straining for footsteps. She wrote at the library, head bent low, shielding the pages with her arm. She wrote in her head while scrubbing dishes, while folding laundry, while lying in bed listening to the floorboards creak under Darryl's weight. Her stories became her rebellion, her secret heartbeat.

But shadows followed her, even there. In the mirror, she saw a girl with tired eyes, sleeves pulled down over thin wrists, lips pressed into silence. She wondered if her father would have recognized her. She wondered if he would have loved her enough to listen.

And, time moved everything forward. The Whitaker house sagged deeper into itself, the smell of mildew heavier, the clutter multiplying until it felt like living inside a landfill of broken promises. Abby's bottles clinked in the trash, Darryl's sneers grew sharper, and Cassandra wrote herself doorways that never opened.

And still, she kept the razor in her sock drawer—not because she longed for death, but because sometimes she needed the sting of proof that she was still alive.

The Fall of Darryl

When Darryl turned twenty-five, the Whitaker house had begun to feel too small to hold his restless anger. He moved through it like a caged animal, pacing, snarling, leaving dents in the plaster where his fists landed after an argument with Abby. His voice deepened, his body thickened with muscle from years of odd jobs and careless fights, but his eyes held the same sharp glint they always had—the glint of a boy who had decided cruelty was safer than weakness.

He took a job at Lehigh Lumber Mill, one of the few steady employers in the valley. The mill sat at the edge of town, its corrugated metal siding dulled by years of sawdust and weather. The air around it always carried a fine grit of pine, sweet and acrid all at once, settling on cars and coats, clinging to the hair of every man who worked there. It was brutal work—splitting, stacking, sorting—but it came with a paycheck, and in Carbon County, that was enough to mark a man respectable.

Darryl liked the paycheck, but he liked the feel of easy money more. He discovered early that it was simple to skim: a little off the top here, a few falsified hours there, supplies "borrowed" and sold in the next county. He thought himself clever, invisible. But cleverness wasn't one of Darryl's gifts; arrogance was. He bragged in bars, flashed cash he hadn't earned, bought rounds he couldn't afford. People noticed. People always notice.

Back at the Whitaker house, Abby puffed herself up with pride, telling anyone who'd listen that her boy was finally making something of himself. "Darryl's got a job at the mill," she'd say between drags of her cigarette, chin tilted high. "Good money. Honest work. He'll take care of me now."

Cassandra kept her silence. She saw the bills crumpled in Darryl's pocket, the way he slipped them out with a flourish, the way his eyes darted around the room as if checking to see who envied him. She saw the arrogance harden in his posture, the swagger in his step. She knew better than to believe her brother had turned a corner. Men like Darryl didn't change; they only found new ways to sharpen their edges.

It was late autumn when it happened, the air sharp with the smell of woodsmoke and damp leaves. Cassandra was fifteen, balancing schoolwork with her endless writing, her spiral notebooks stacked in careful towers under her bed. She came home one evening to find Abby pacing the kitchen, cigarette clutched between two trembling fingers, ash scattering on the linoleum.

"They've arrested him," Abby hissed the moment Cassandra stepped through the door. Her eyes were wide, frantic, the whites streaked red. "Your brother. They say he's been stealing. From the mill. Can you believe that? My boy, a thief?"

Cassandra stood frozen in the doorway, her schoolbag slipping down her shoulder. She wanted to say yes. She wanted to say she believed it entirely, that it was the only outcome that had ever made sense. But she bit her tongue, as she always did, and let Abby rant.

"They've got it wrong," Abby muttered, pacing. "Someone set him up. Someone jealous, that's what it is. People can't stand to see us Whitakers doing well. Always waiting for us to fall."

But the papers told another story. Lehigh Lumber Mill Employee Charged in Theft Scheme. The article laid it out in cold print: falsified time sheets, missing supplies, cash transactions traced back to Darryl. Eighteen months in Carbon County Correctional Facility.

Abby tore the newspaper in half, then into shreds, as though destroying the story would change the truth. She smoked through half a pack that evening, muttering curses at the neighbours, at the mill, at the judge, at the world. Finally, she turned her fury toward Cassandra.

"This is your fault," she spat, pointing a trembling finger. "You've always hated him. Always wished him gone. You jinxed him, didn't you? All that scribbling, all those lies—you brought this on your brother."

Cassandra felt the words like stones hurled at her chest. She wanted to scream, to shout that Darryl had earned every day of his sentence, and more, that he had hurt her in ways their mother refused to see. But she swallowed it down, let it settle heavy in her stomach, and said nothing. Truth, she had already learned, was useless here.

When Darryl was taken away, the house exhaled for the first time in years, and so did Cassandra. It wasn't freedom, not fully—Abby still prowled the rooms with her smoke and her bitterness—but it was reprieve. The shadows stretched differently without him. Cassandra no longer tensed at every creak of the floorboards, no longer feared the sound of his laughter as he crawled beneath her covers.

At night, she wrote more feverishly, her flashlight flickering under the blanket as she filled notebook after notebook. Her stories grew darker, sharper, dripping with monsters who were finally banished, at least for a time. She wrote of girls who built cages for their tormentors, who locked them away where their laughter could no longer reach. She wrote of silence not as punishment, but as peace.

Still, Abby would not let her forget. "Your brother's a good boy," she said one night, her words slurred with liquor. "He's just misunderstood. Not like you, with your scribbles and your sulks. At least he tries."

Cassandra nodded, as she always did, and retreated to her room. There, she lay awake, the weight of relief tangled with guilt. She was glad he was gone—glad in a way that felt dangerous, almost sinful. She savoured the quiet, the space, the absence of dread. But she knew it was temporary. Eighteen months was a reprieve, not a pardon.

The Whitaker house sagged deeper into itself, its siding peeling, its windows smudged with smoke. The smell of mildew grew sharper, the clutter heavier. Abby's rage filled the rooms, bouncing off the walls until it became the air Cassandra breathed.

But for the first time, Cassandra could breathe without choking. For the first time, the house did not hold two predators. For the first time, silence was not just survival but sanctuary.

And she wrote. God, she wrote.

The Last Page of Childhood

The winter Darryl came home from jail was one of the coldest Cassandra could remember. The snow clung to the steep Jim Thorpe streets until March, salt-stained cars grinding their way up and down Broadway, the Lehigh River locked under a crust of ice. Cassandra was seventeen then, her body stretched into the awkward beauty of young womanhood, her mind already sharpening into escape.

She dreaded the sound of her brother's boots on the porch again, the creak of the door, the swagger in his voice. But when Darryl was released, he didn't come home. Instead, he moved in with a man he'd met inside— Paul, older by a decade, and Paul's wife, Sandy. Their house was a sagging duplex on the edge of Nesquehoning, and for reasons Cassandra never asked, they welcomed Darryl into their cluttered orbit.

Abby told it as though it were proof of his worth. "See?" she crowed, cigarette bobbing between her fingers. "Even in jail, people can see Darryl's a good man. He makes friends everywhere."

Cassandra said nothing. Relief hummed in her chest like a secret hymn. With Darryl gone, the house was different—not quiet exactly, but less painful, less dangerous. The shadows stretched longer without his presence, but they were softer, easier to live with. She no longer slept with her body rigid, braced against the sound of his footsteps in the hall. The reprieve was fragile, but it was hers.

Abby filled the empty space with her own bitterness. Without Darryl to lean on, she turned her full attention back to Cassandra, her words cutting deeper, her hand quicker to strike.

"You think you're better than me," she sneered one night when Cassandra returned from the library, arms full of borrowed books. "Parading around with your nose in those things. You think you'll leave this town and forget where you came from? Newsflash—you can't outrun blood. You're a Whitaker, and Whitakers don't get out."

Cassandra swallowed her retorts, slipped into her room, and wrote until her fingers cramped.

By then, writing was no longer just escape—it was sustenance. She had filled dozens of notebooks, their pages bristling with half-finished stories, monsters, ghosts and terrors that had been all too real in her life. But in the last year, something had shifted. Her stories began to grow longer, more intricate. She traced her characters from childhood to adulthood, built towns that looked suspiciously like Jim Thorpe, planted forests haunted by whispers she knew too well.

The story that emerged was darker than anything she had written before. It centred on a girl named Eliza who lived in a house that breathed like a predator, walls groaning, floorboards whispering secrets. Eliza's family denied the shadows that curled around her bed at night, insisting she was imagining things. But the monsters were real—too real—and Eliza's greatest horror was not the creatures themselves but the silence of those who refused to see.

Cassandra poured herself into Eliza. Every bruise, every truth cover up, every silenced plea bled into the pages. She wrote until dawn sometimes, the words spilling faster than her hand could catch them. When her flashlight batteries died, she scribbled by the pale wash of moonlight.

The manuscript grew heavy under her hands. She bought cheap binders from the five-and-dime and filled them with loose-leaf paper, her handwriting cramped and slanted, margins scrawled with corrections. She titled it *The Shadows of Ashfield*.

The name came from the way the mountains loomed at dusk, casting the town in darkness long before the sun truly set. But it was also something else—something inside her, a recognition that her life had been one long shadow she was trying to step out of.

When she turned eighteen that spring, Cassandra held the finished manuscript in her hands. It was thicker than any of her notebooks, heavier than any burden she had ever carried, and yet it felt a lot like freedom.

On the night of her birthday, Abby barely acknowledged her. A muttered "happy now?" as she shoved a slice of store-bought cake across the table, the frosting smeared and lopsided. Cassandra ate in silence, the sweetness turning to paste in her mouth.

Later, in her room, she spread the manuscript across her bed. The pages rippled in uneven stacks, some smudged with ink, others wrinkled from sweat or tears. She traced her fingers along the title she had written on the first page, her handwriting jagged but certain.

This was hers. Not Abby's. Not Darryl's. Not even the house's. Hers.

She stared at it for a long time, listening to the creaks of the house settling around her, the sigh of wind through the cracked window frame, the muffled sound of Abby's cough through the wall. She thought of her father —of the life she never got to know, of the light that went out before she could see it. She thought of her brother—of the way his laughter still haunted her bones. She thought of her mother—of the venom, the hands, the endless chorus of *you'll never be anything.*

And she thought of herself—of the girl in the mirror who no longer looked away.

Eighteen years old, manuscript in hand, Cassandra made a vow.

She would leave Jim Thorpe. She would leave the mildew-soaked house, the cigarette smoke, the whispers, the ghosts. She would carve a new life out of the wreckage, write herself into existence somewhere no one could tell her she was nothing.

She pressed the manuscript to her chest and closed her eyes. *The Shadows of Ashfield* might never be read, never leave the confines of her room—but it had carried her here, to the threshold of freedom.

Part II
The Compass of Morality

Twenty years later, Cassandra Whitaker—though the world did not know her by that name—sat at her desk in a house where silence meant peace, not danger.

The home perched on a bluff above Alki Point, its windows flung wide to the restless breath of Puget Sound. From her writing room, she could see the water spread out like hammered silver, the ferries crossing slow and steady between the peninsulas, the Olympic Mountains rearing jagged and snowcapped beyond. It was a view she never took for granted. Each morning, she carried her coffee to the window, watching the gulls wheel and shriek overhead, the tide curling in and out as if reminding her that everything, even the hardest things, could shift.

She had built a life here, brick by brick, word by word. The girl who once hid notebooks beneath her bed now commanded shelves lined with hardcovers stamped with her pen name: Leigh Smith. Critics called her "the queen of literary horror," her books dissected in university seminars, her characters tattooed on the arms of readers who swore they saw themselves in her ghosts.

Her writing room reflected that double life—both scholar and dreamer. One wall held floor-to-ceiling bookshelves, each packed with first editions she'd hunted for across the years: Shirley Jackson's *The Haunting of Hill House*, Daphne du Maurier's *Rebecca*, a worn copy of Stephen King's *Pet Sematary* with the original dust jacket frayed at the edges. Between the classics stood her own works, their spines uniform and stark, as though daring to belong beside them.

The opposite wall was almost entirely glass. Sunlight poured through on clear days, shifting across her desk, illuminating the papers scattered there. The sound of the water carried through, a hush and crash that had become her metronome. When she wrote, she matched her breath to its rhythm, as if the sea itself carried her stories.

Behind her, pinned to corkboards and taped to walls, were scraps of her process: maps of fictional towns, photographs of abandoned houses, scribbled notes that only she could decipher. It was chaos, but it was hers, and she had learned that creation often lived best in disorder.

In the next room, laughter rose—her daughters, twin voices tumbling over each other like stones in a river. Eve and Eden were eleven, identical down to the dimple in their left cheeks, but their personalities stretched in opposite directions. Eve was the dreamer, always with a book under her arm, her mind wandering as easily as her mother's once had, though for very different reasons. Eden was the anchor, sharp-eyed, quick to notice when something was amiss. They were halves of a whole, each carrying a piece of Cassandra she had thought too broken to pass down.

Owen's voice followed, warm and steady, coaxing the girls toward breakfast. He was a West Coast native, tall and unhurried, with a patience that sometimes startled her. A former architect who had set aside his career to raise their daughters when her books began to climb the bestseller lists, Owen carried domestic life with a grace that made it seem like art. He cooked with devotion, folded laundry with a kind of reverence, tended the girls' scraped knees as though each bandage was an act of love.

Sometimes, when she watched him move through their home, Cassandra felt the ache of disbelief. That she had escaped Jim Thorpe. That she had built this life. That she could write terror on the page while living in a house where love was not conditional, where the people closest to her did not turn away from her truth.

She carried her coffee to the desk and set it beside her laptop, the screen still glowing with the half-finished paragraph from last night's work. Outside, a freighter groaned across the Sound, its low horn rolling like thunder. She closed her eyes, inhaled, and let herself feel it—the steadiness of the sea, the warmth of her home, the absence of fear.

Yet the past never vanished entirely. It lived in her still, a shadow curled under her ribs. Sometimes, when Owen's voice rose—not in anger but simply to call across the house—her body tensed before her mind reminded her it was safe. Sometimes, when Eve or Eden slammed a door in childish frustration, Cassandra's chest tightened with echoes of slammed doors that meant something else entirely.

She wrote because of those shadows. Every story was a way to lay them down, to shape them into something she could understand. Readers often wrote in forums, asking why her novels always circled back to haunted houses, to families fractured by secrets, to girls who screamed the truth only to find no one listening. Cassandra, who had never outed herself as the pen behind Leigh Smith, was grateful she would never have to answer this question.

Leigh Smith was her shield. Cassandra Whitaker was the ghost who had lived in the Whitaker house. Leigh Smith was the woman the world applauded. And she guarded that separation fiercely.

The twins burst into her office without knocking, their hair still tangled from sleep, mismatched pajamas brushing their ankles. "Mom!" Eve cried, holding up a notebook. "Can you read my story?"

Eden rolled her eyes. "It's about a horse that talks. Again."

"It's about more than that," Eve insisted, thrusting the notebook toward Cassandra. "It's about magic."

Cassandra smiled, taking the pages in her hand. The handwriting slanted, uneven, letters pressing too close together. She remembered her own notebooks, the ones she had hidden beneath her bed, the ones filled with monsters that looked too much like home. She glanced at her daughter's eager face and felt her throat tighten with gratitude. Eve's monsters lived in talking horses and enchanted forests, not in the hallways of their house.

"It's beautiful," Cassandra said softly, and meant it.

Eden crossed her arms, though a smile tugged at her lips. "She never finishes them. You always say you will, but you don't."

Eve stuck out her tongue. Cassandra laughed, pulling them both close, inhaling the scent of them, the faint salt of the sea clinging to their hair. These girls were her proof—proof that cycles could be broken, that new legacies could be written.

When Owen called them back to the kitchen, promising pancakes with too much syrup, Cassandra watched them leave and let the silence settle again. The Sound rolled steady, gulls shrieked, the house creaked in its bones. She turned back to her desk, placed her hands on the keyboard, and began to write.

This was the life she had built. A house filled with laughter instead of rage. A marriage held together by love. Children who lived without fear. A career that allowed her to shape her pain into art.

A Message in the Dark

It began with a flicker—an ordinary night, the twins asleep, Owen rinsing dishes in the kitchen, Cassandra scrolling absentmindedly through her latest novel on her laptop in her writing room. The Sound was calm, the tide hushed and silver under the moon. She was half-tuned to the rhythm of water against stone, that eternal breathing she had come to rely on, when the screen shifted.

A notification.

She frowned. She didn't keep a personal Facebook account. She never had. Leigh Smith maintained a page—carefully managed by her publicist, curated with book releases, tour dates, occasional photographs carefully photoshopped to look like someone else. The account was untraceable to Cassandra Whitaker. That was the point.

Yet here it was. An iMessage from an unknown number with the area code 570.

At first she thought it must be a fan who had slipped through some crack in the firewall, someone determined enough to dig. It happened, rarely. She hovered over the message, debating whether to ignore it, when the sender next sent their name.

Darryl Whitaker.

Her stomach dropped.

She hadn't seen the name in decades. Hadn't heard his voice in longer. The letters themselves felt invasive, as though they had crawled through a locked door. She closed her eyes, inhaled once, slow, steady. *It's nothing,* she told herself. It's just a name on a screen. *He doesn't know where you are. He can't touch you here.*

But when she clicked, the message bloomed like rot:

Cass its me. Been long time. I woudnt msg if it wasnt bad. Mom real bad. She fell hit her hed. Docs say her brain dont work rite no more. I tryin take care of her but its too much for me. Need help.

Her hands trembled on the keys. The words swam.

Mom.
Fall.
Brain damage.

A chill ran the length of her spine.

The room seemed smaller suddenly, the shelves closing in, the sea beyond the window hushed into nothing. She read the message again, slower this time, her mind clawing at the implications.

She hadn't seen Abby in twenty years. Hadn't spoken to her since the day she left Jim Thorpe. She had built an entire life on the absence of her mother and brother. And now, with a handful of broken sentences, the absence cracked open.

Behind her, Owen's footsteps padded down the hall. He leaned into the doorway, drying his hands on a towel. "You okay?"

Cassandra shut the laptop too quickly. The sound was sharp, final.

"Fine," she said. Her voice was steady, but the lie trembled beneath it.

Owen tilted his head, reading her the way he always did, but he didn't press. He crossed the room, kissed the top of her head, and said he'd be in bed when she was ready. His warmth lingered, but it couldn't soften the chill that had settled into her bones.

When he was gone, she opened the laptop again. The message still glowed, waiting.

Her first instinct was to delete it. To block him. To pretend it had never arrived. But the words clung, needling. *Mom real bad. Docs say her brain dont work rite no more. Need help.*

She sat back in her chair, eyes fixed on the glass of the window. Her reflection hovered there—older now, lined at the edges, but still carrying the shadows of the girl who had once begged to be believed. Behind her, the sea stretched endless, indifferent.

The Compass Points East

The message stayed in her chest like a splinter. All night it lodged there, sharp and nagging, no matter how many times she told herself to ignore it. By morning, Cassandra had read Darryl's words a dozen times, memorized their cadence, their false warmth. She needs you. The phrase burrowed under her ribs.

At breakfast, the kitchen filled with the ordinary sounds of their life: Eve humming as she buttered toast, Eden arguing that syrup belonged on pancakes and nowhere else, Owen's steady hands flipping eggs in the skillet. The sea glimmered beyond the windows, gulls shrieking in the wind, the world carrying on in its familiar rhythm. But Cassandra sat at the table, the message still pulsing behind her eyes.

She cleared her throat. "I need to tell you all something."

Owen looked up, spatula paused mid-air. The girls stilled, sensing a shift in the room. Cassandra folded her hands on the table, the way she used to before speaking in class, when she wanted her voice to sound braver than she felt.

"Your uncle Darryl messaged me," she said carefully.

The words dropped into the room like stones into still water. Ripples spread across their faces—confusion on the girls', concern on Owen's.

"How did he get your number?" Eden said, her brow furrowing.

"I don't. But that's not what's important," Cassandra began.

Owen set the spatula down, the eggs forgotten. "So, what did he say?"

Cassandra exhaled. "He said... Mom's sick. That she had a fall, or something like that. Brain damage. That he's been trying to take care of her but can't manage it alone." She paused, pressing her palms flat against the wood grain of the table. "He said she needs me."

Silence stretched. Outside, the tide crashed against the rocks, steady and unrelenting.

Eve was the first to speak. "Grandma's sick?" Her eyes widened, curious, cautious. "We've never met her. Can we?"

Eden frowned. "We know she's been mean to Mom, why should we?"

Cassandra's heart ached at the simplicity of their reasoning. They had only ever known kindness, the safety of a home where love was given freely. They didn't understand the weight of cruelty when it came from the people meant to protect you.

"She was..." Cassandra searched for the right word. "Difficult. She hurt me in ways a mother shouldn't. That's why I left Jim Thorpe. That's why I never took you back." This wasn't the first time she had told her daughters some of the story of where she came from, but it was the first time it felt like that past was breathing down her neck.

The girls exchanged glances, a silent conversation only twins could hold. Then Eve said softly, "But she's still your mom."

The words cut clean. Yes. She was still Cassandra's mother. A woman who had bruised her, silenced her, denied her truth—but still, mother.

Owen pulled out a chair and sat across from her, his gaze steady. "Cass," he said quietly, using the nickname he alone had permission to. "You don't owe them anything. Not her. Not him. You built this life with me for a reason."

"I know." Her voice wavered. "But if she really is sick... if she really can't take care of herself... what kind of person would I be if I ignored that? The right thing is the right thing, Owen. It has to be. Otherwise what's the point of everything?"

He reached across the table, covering her hands with his. His skin was warm, grounding. "I'll support whatever you decide. But I need you to be sure this is about what's right—and not about old guilt sneaking back in."

Cassandra's throat tightened. How could she explain the compass inside her, the one that always pointed toward obligation no matter how jagged the path? She had spent her life being punished for telling the truth, for trying to do the right thing. If she turned away now, what would that make her?

"I need to go," she whispered. "If for no other reason, just to see. Just to know." Then she turned to her daughters. "But I need to go alone."

The girls protested, voices rising in a twin chorus. "We want to come! We want to meet her!"

Cassandra shook her head, firm but gentle. "No. Not yet. This is something I need to face myself first. If it's safe, if it feels right, then maybe later. But not now."

Their faces fell, but they didn't argue. They trusted her, even when they didn't understand.

After breakfast, Cassandra stood at the window of her writing room, watching the ferries crawl across the Sound. The sky was pewter, the water restless, gulls dipping low before vanishing into the mist. She pressed her palm to the glass and whispered to her reflection, "The right thing is the right thing."

Behind her, the shelves of first editions loomed, her own books lined neatly beside them. Evidence of the life she had built—words spun from silence, stories carved from wounds. She thought of the girl she had been, sitting in a library in Jim Thorpe, scribbling into spiral notebooks, dreaming of escape. That girl had vowed never to return.

And yet, here she was.

She packed lightly: jeans, sweaters, notebooks. She slid The Shadows of Ashfield—her first manuscript, battered but still whole—into the bottom of her suitcase. Not because she would need it, but because it reminded her who she had been, and how far she had come.

That night, as Owen lay beside her in the dark, he whispered, "Promise me you'll be careful."

"I promise."

He kissed her temple. "And promise me you'll come back."

Cassandra closed her eyes, listening to the sea beating steady against the shore. "I'll always come back," she murmured. But in her chest, doubt coiled tight, whispering that going home was never as simple as returning.

In the morning, the compass inside her pointed east.

And she followed.

The House of Rot

The drive east carried her through landscapes that felt both familiar and foreign. The Cascades gave way to plains, the plains to mountains again, until finally the old ridges of Pennsylvania rose up in their muted greens and browns. Jim Thorpe appeared at the bend of the Lehigh River, its narrow streets squeezed between slopes, brick buildings clinging stubbornly to the hillside. To outsiders, the town was picturesque, a postcard of Victorian facades and tourist shops. But Cassandra knew better. Beauty was a veneer; rot lived in the cracks.

She parked a rented sedan at the foot of the street she had once walked every day as a child. The Whitaker house stood where it always had, though time had not been kind. The porch sagged, its boards warped and splintered, the railing leaning as though exhausted. Siding peeled in long strips, exposing wood swollen with damp. The windows were clouded, curtains yellowed with years of smoke. Even from the sidewalk, she caught the stench—urine, mould, something sweet and rotten layered beneath.

Her chest tightened. The house had always been heavy, but now it seemed malignant, a living organism collapsing under the weight of its own decay.

She mounted the porch carefully, testing each step before shifting her weight. The door still bore the scar where Bill's boots used to kick mud off before entering, though now it was warped, paint blistered, the knob rusted. She turned it. Unlocked.

The smell hit her first. Stale smoke and ammonia, mould and unwashed skin. It wrapped around her like a damp shroud, thick enough to taste. She swallowed hard and stepped inside.

The living room was a ruin. Furniture sagged, cushions stained, springs jutting through fabric. Ashtrays overflowed on every surface, cigarette butts spilling onto the carpet, ground into the fibres. Bottles lined the floor like soldiers fallen in battle. The wallpaper peeled in strips, exposing plaster mottled with black mould.

And in the middle of it all, Abby sat in her old armchair, a queen on a throne of ruin.

Her hair, once dark and thick, had thinned into greasy grey strands that stuck to her forehead. Her skin was sallow, eyes clouded, but her posture still carried something defiant, something that refused to break even as her body failed her. She looked at Cassandra and laughed.

"My brain is scrambled eggs," she announced, voice cracking. Then, without pause, she shifted. "Did you see the dog in the yard? He said he'd fix the roof, but the roof won't stay put, no, no, no."

Her words spilled like broken glass, jagged and senseless.

"Mom," Cassandra whispered, stepping closer.

Abby's eyes sharpened for a flicker, focusing. "Cassie?" Then, just as quickly, she slipped again. "Cassie took the bus, bus, bus to Scranton. Bus driver's name was John. He told me the numbers don't add up. Did you pay the man? Did you? Did you?"

Cassandra's throat closed. She wanted to kneel, to take her mother's hand, to summon tenderness she wasn't sure she had. Instead she stood frozen, watching the wreckage of the woman who had raised her, who had broken her, who had never once believed her.

A knock startled her.

She turned to find a man in uniform at the door—a local police officer, broad-shouldered, his cap in his hand. He stepped inside, wrinkling his nose at the smell.

"Didn't expect to find anyone here," he said, glancing at Cassandra. "You are?"

"Her daughter," Cassandra answered. The words felt foreign on her tongue.

His brows lifted. "Daughter? Well, I'll be damned. I've been checking in on her for years and never knew she had kids."

The statement landed like a blow. Years? Darryl had made this all sound recent. Never knew she had kids? As if Abby had erased them, or chosen not to speak of them, or perhaps simply forgotten. Cassandra wasn't sure which was worse.

"She wanders," the officer explained. "I've picked her up more times than I can count—out in the streets, barefoot in the middle of winter, once halfway to Nesquehoning. Usually I bring her back here, make sure she's not hurt."

He removed his cap and extended his hand. "I'm Brady," he said by way of introduction.

"Cassandra," she reached out and shook his hand. "I'm here from Washington."

Cassandra's stomach knotted. "My brother said she had a fall," she began. "But he made it sound recent?"

The officer frowned. "Fall? No. That's not what happened." Brady shifted his weight, his expression tightening. "Three years ago, she was brought into the hospital. Head trauma. The kind you don't get from tripping on a sidewalk. She told us she'd been hit. Assaulted in her home. But by the time we tried to follow up, she wouldn't—or couldn't—say by who. And we never found the guy."

The room tilted. Cassandra gripped the back of a chair, the rot soft under her fingers.

"Assaulted," she repeated, her voice flat.

"That's right." The officer looked at her more closely. "Whoever told you it was a fall wasn't telling you the truth."

Cassandra thought of Darryl's message, his casual words, his plea for help. She thought of his smirk all those years ago when Abby had chosen his word over hers. Her stomach churned with dread and certainty.

Brady his cap back on his head. "Anyway, I'll keep checking in. But if you're here for a while, maybe she's got a better shot." He gave a small nod and left, pulling the door shut behind him.

Silence filled the house again, broken only by Abby's babble: "Bus, bus, scrambled eggs, numbers don't add up, Cassie Cassie Cassie."

Cassandra stood in the ruins of her childhood, the truth clawing at her throat. She had come here for clarity, for some clean line between past and present. Instead, she found only rot—the house, her mother's mind, the lies her brother spun.

And in that moment, she understood: the compass pointing her home was not leading her to answers. It was leading her deeper into the shadows she thought she'd left behind.

The First Threads Unravel

The Whitaker house pressed on her chest like a weight. Every hour spent there left her lungs tighter, her skin carrying the stench of smoke and rot that clung no matter how often she scrubbed her hands. Abby's babble filled the rooms—half-words, fragments of memory, phrases that circled and devoured themselves like snakes eating their own tails. Cassandra kept a notebook open, writing down the things her mother said in case a pattern might emerge. None ever did.

But beneath the incoherence, Cassandra felt something pulsing. A lie. A silence. A wrongness that needed naming.

The first thread tugged loose with the car.

She found the registration in a drawer, buried under layers of unopened mail, overdue notices, and pizza coupons yellowed with grease. The paper was folded, creased so many times it nearly fell apart in her hands. Her mother's name had once been typed neatly across the top: Abigail Whitaker. But now, beneath it, a transfer of ownership scribbled in ballpoint ink: Darryl Whitaker.

Cassandra sat back in the sagging armchair, the smell of mildew rising from the cushion, her hands trembling around the page. From other papers Cassandra had found, she knew Abby had driven a 2018 Honda CR-V, bought with the settlement from a car accident years ago. It had been her one reliable possession, something she boasted of to anyone who would listen. And now it belonged to Darryl.

When she confronted him on the phone, his voice oozed false innocence.

"Yeah, I took over the car," he admitted, tone light, almost casual. "Mom didn't need it anymore. Wasn't safe for her to drive, not with her head the way it is. Figured I'd keep it in the family. Wendy traded it in for something newer—better mileage, you know? It's fine, Cass. Don't get all bent out of shape."

Her jaw tightened. "She paid for that car. With her own money. It wasn't yours to take, and from what I am seeing here, she needs money. She could have sold it."

He chuckled. "God, you're dramatic. You always were. Mom agreed to it. Ask her yourself if you don't believe me. She wanted me and Wendy to have it."

She closed her eyes, picturing Abby rocking in her chair, muttering about scrambled eggs and bus rides. Mom agreed to it.The words were ash in her mouth.

The second thread came with the deed.

The police officer's words about the "assault" gnawed at her until she couldn't sleep. One morning, she drove into town, the road curling past the old courthouse with its clock tower looming like a judge above the streets. Inside the records office, the air smelled of paper and dust, the hum of fluorescent lights filling the silence.

"Property records for 214 Maple," she told the clerk. Her voice trembled, though she tried to keep it steady.

The woman shuffled papers, tapped keys on a sluggish computer, and returned with a thin folder. Cassandra opened it with trembling fingers.

The deed was there, stamped and notarized. Three years ago, Abby had signed the house over to Darryl. No sale price, just a transfer of ownership, the signature shaky but legible.

Cassandra stared at it until the letters blurred. This house, this rotting cage, had been Abby's anchor, her only real possession. And Darryl had taken it.

The third thread was the bank.

She drove Abby downtown, coaxing her into the passenger seat with promises of coffee and fresh air. Abby mumbled nonsense the entire way, her eyes darting from window to window as though she recognized ghosts on every corner. At the branch of PNC Bank, the teller smiled politely, though her eyes lingered on Abby with pity.

"I'd like to review my mother's account," Cassandra said, producing the faded chequebook she had found in the drawer.

The teller hesitated. "Is she present?"

Abby waved vaguely at the counter. "Numbers don't add up, scrambled eggs, eggs, eggs."

"Yes," Cassandra said softly. "She's here."

The teller nodded and tapped the keyboard. "It appears your mother's account is joint—with someone named Darryl Whitaker."

Cassandra felt her stomach drop. "Joint?"

"Yes. Her account is actually overdrawn. And the withdrawals—" The teller frowned at the screen. "Almost all are cash. ATM withdrawals from his card. Regular, frequent."

Cassandra closed her eyes, fighting the urge to slam her fist against the counter. Her SSI. Her Medicaid. Every dollar meant for her care drained into his pockets.

That night, she called Darryl again.

"I saw the account," she said without preamble. "You've drained it. All of it."

On the other end, silence. Then a sigh. "Look, I didn't want to tell you like this, but yeah. I've got a problem. Gambling. Always have, you know that. It got bad. The house payments fell behind. I had to remortgage. It's out of control."

"Out of control?" Cassandra's voice cracked. "You stole from her. You stole her house. Her car. Her money. Everything she had."

"Don't be so high and mighty," Darryl snapped. "You ran off and left us. I was the one here, dealing with her, watching her go downhill. You don't know what it's like. I did what I had to do."

"You did what you wanted to do," she shot back. "And now you want me to clean it up."

He hesitated. "Cass... just cover the mortgage payments, okay? I'll get back on my feet. I swear. I'll fix it."

"No," she whispered, the word tasting like iron. "No," she said again, more firmly.

When the call ended, she sat in the dark, Abby babbling from the other room, the house groaning with its age. She dialed the police, voice trembling as she laid out everything: the car, the house, the account, the theft. The officer took her statement, promised to look into it. She clung to that promise like a lifeline.

Days passed. Nothing happened.

The house remained in Darryl's name. The account remained overdrawn. The car was long gone. Abby sat in her chair, muttering nonsense, her mind fractured beyond repair.

Truth had never been enough in this family. Not when she was a child. Not now.

But Cassandra was not that child anymore. She would not be silenced again.

The next week, she drove to the courthouse and filed the paperwork for conservatorship. The clerk behind the counter raised her brows, sliding the forms across. "You'll have to notify your brother," she said.

Cassandra gripped the pen tight, her name carving into the paper with deliberate strokes. "I know."

As she signed, she felt the compass in her chest settle. The right thing was the right thing, even when it cost her.

The first threads had unraveled. And she was ready to follow them into the dark.

Part III
Burn the Witch

The Lies in the Courthouse

The courthouse in Jim Thorpe had always looked like a fortress. Built of red sandstone, its Romanesque arches loomed over the narrow streets, its clock tower watching the valley like a stern guardian. As a girl, Cassandra had walked past it holding her breath, convinced the stone lions at the entrance could sniff out guilt, even where none exists. Now, at thirty-eight, she climbed its steps again, her file of documents pressed to her chest, and felt the same childhood dread pressing down on her.

She had come with truth. Proof of Darryl's thefts: the car, the house, the drained account. The papers were heavy in her folder, their weight reassuring. But the moment she stepped into the echoing chamber of the Carbon County courthouse, truth seemed suddenly small against the shadows of history, of bias, of all the ways the system bent toward the loudest voices and those who had lived here long enough to be believed without question.

Darryl and Wendy had filed their petition to contest her bid for conservatorship. The first time she read it, sitting at Abby's cluttered kitchen table with the stink of mould in her nose, her hands had gone numb. Line after line carved into her like knives.

Cassandra Anderson (nee Whitaker) is abusive toward her mother. She has been absent for twenty years and returned only in pursuit of financial gain.
She has a history of mental instability, self-harm, and erratic behaviour.
She is emotionally unfit to serve as conservator.

They had gathered the bones of her childhood, combined them with fabrication, and twisted them into a weapon.

She sat in the courtroom as the judge shuffled papers, his glasses slipping down his nose, his tone weary as though every case before him blurred into the same grey smear. The wood-paneled walls smelled of varnish and dust, the air too warm, the clock ticking too loudly above their heads.

Wendy sat beside Darryl, her posture stiff but her eyes gleaming. She wore a pale blouse buttoned to the collar, her hair smoothed into something respectable. Darryl, by contrast, looked almost casual—shirt sleeves rolled, a tie knotted poorly, his smirk tugging at the corner of his mouth. He leaned back in his chair like a man who already knew the outcome, his eyes flicking toward Cassandra with lazy cruelty.

When their lawyer spoke, Cassandra felt her pulse hammer in her ears.

"Your Honour," the woman began, her voice sweetened with false concern. "My clients only want what is best for their mother. They have been here, consistently, caring for her day in and day out, while Cassandra has been absent for two decades. Now, suddenly, she reappears—not out of love, but to gain control of her mother's property and finances. Their mother herself has described Cassandra as cruel and neglectful."

Cassandra's hands clenched around her folder. Abby's babble echoed in her memory—scrambled eggs, bus rides, nonsense. That was not testimony. That was incoherence. And yet here it was, Abby's voice, weaponized against her.

The lawyer continued: "There is evidence—" she glanced down at her notes, though Cassandra knew there wasn't any evidence at all "—that Cassandra has a long history of instability. Self-harming, erratic disappearances, and a fixation on horror writing that suggests she cannot distinguish reality from fiction. She is, quite frankly, unfit."

The words echoed off the high ceiling, staining the air. Cassandra wanted to rise, to shout, to tear the lies apart one by one. But her lawyer, a local man with thinning hair and tired eyes, placed a hand on her arm. "Wait," he murmured. "Your turn will come."

When it came, her voice shook. Her lawyer laid out the evidence: the car transferred to Darryl, the deed signed under suspicious circumstances, the drained account. He explained the pattern of gambling, of neglect, of theft. He spoke of Brady, the police officer who had confirmed her mother was assaulted. Abby had not fallen.

But even as he spoke, Cassandra saw it—the doubt in the judge's eyes, the impatience in his sighs. Cassandra was not local anymore. She was a stranger. Outsiders always spoke too well, dressed too neatly, looked too polished for Jim Thorpe's comfort.

Darryl's lies, though thinner than smoke, clung easier in the judge's mind because they fit the story everyone in town already believed: that Cassandra had left, and Darryl had stayed.

Truth bent beneath the weight of familiarity.

The hearing ended with no ruling, only continuance. "I'll need more time," the judge said, already turning to the next file. "Court will reconvene in six weeks."

Six weeks. An eternity.

Outside, the air was sharp with winter. Cassandra stood on the courthouse steps, her folder pressed tight to her chest, her breath clouding white. Darryl and Wendy brushed past her, their laughter low but deliberate.

"See you next time, sis," Darryl murmured, his smirk slicing across his face like a blade.

Wendy's perfume lingered in the air after they passed, cloying and false.

Cassandra closed her eyes. The compass in her chest spun wildly, its needle pulling her in two directions at once—back to Washing, to safety and love, or deeper into Jim Thorpe's shadows, where lies multiplied faster than truth.

When she opened her eyes again, the courthouse loomed above her, indifferent, its clock tower ticking away the time she did not have.

She whispered into the wind, barely audible: "The right thing is the right thing."

And though her voice trembled, she knew she would stay.

The Arrival of the Anchor

Owen arrived in Jim Thorpe on a day the valley wore a pewter sky. The mountains crouched like sleeping animals, the river a dull band of steel threading the town. Cassandra stood beneath the portico of the inn on Broadway, collar turned up against the wind that slipped off the Lehigh and slid under clothes with a wet, insinuating chill. She watched the airport shuttle turn the corner, past the courthouse that still looked like a sermon carved in stone, and felt her stomach loosen for the first time in days.

He stepped down with his little duffel, the fabric darkened by mist. Even from a distance, she could map the familiar geography of him—shoulders that had carried the twins through fevers and first days of school, hands that could coax a soup to taste like memory. He lifted a hand, a small, almost shy wave, and in that gesture was every calm morning of their life, every ordinary grace that had saved her.

When he reached her, they didn't speak at first. They simply folded into each other, that wordless homecoming, his chin against her hair, her face tucked beneath his jaw where she could smell coffee and the wool of his coat and the salt of his skin borne across a continent. The wind shouldered past them and went on down the street. The inn's brass bell chimed as a stranger went in, out, and the town carried on with its errands and rumours.

"I'm here," he said, finally, a breath more than words.

"I know." She stepped back enough to look at him. "How were the girls?"

"Curious. Brave. They wrote you notes for your pillow." He smiled. "Mom's

got them, and they've already talked her into pancakes for supper."
Maggie—Owen's mother—who had once been a midwife and now
cultivated geraniums with the same steady devotion, had flown in from
Victoria, British Columbia to take over the household as though this were
a simple handoff in a relay. "They want to FaceTime before bed. They still
want to meet your mother."

Cassandra nodded. He took her bag—not because she could not carry it,
but because he could—then guided her through the front doors, across
tile that had been scrubbed a century of footsteps thin.

Their room looked toward the ridge line. The bedspread had the floral
insistence of small-town inns everywhere; the radiator clicked and hissed
like an old man clearing his throat. On the dresser, someone had set an
orchard apple in a small bowl, as though a single piece of fruit could pass
for welcome. Owen put his duffel down, then crossed to the window and
pushed back the curtains. The mountains gathered closer, shouldering
the town. In the reflection she saw their two figures—him, solid; her, a little
of the mist still clinging.

He turned, leaned his back against the sill. "Tell me everything," he said.
"Tell me the part you've been trying not to say out loud."

She told him. Not all the way at once—truth rarely travels in a single river,
more often in creeks that find each other. She told him about the house,
how it stank of old smoke and ammonia, as if someone had bottled
despair and spilled it over years. She told him Abby's phrases—my brain is
scrambled eggs—and how they ricocheted between nonsense and ghostly
lucidity, the way a radio sometimes catches a true station for a breath,
then skews to static. She told him about the police officer who had been
checking on her mother because she wandered, and about his face when

he said, Assaulted, not fallen. She told him about the deed, the car, the drained account at PNC, the way Darryl's laugh on the phone had felt like a hand closing round her throat. She told him how the judge sat like a hill unmoved by weather, and how lies had shape-shifted into something nearly legal simply because they were shouted and screamed.

Owen listened without flinching, the way he always had. His silence was not absence; it was the ground holding. At intervals he asked for dates, details, practical edges where action might grip. But mostly he let the words go through him, like tide through pilings, and did not break.

When she had run down, he crossed the room to her and put his palm to the centre of her chest, a touch as light as a benediction. "Right here," he said. "Is it still pointing in the direction you chose?"

She closed her eyes. The compass inside her, that old stubborn instrument, trembled and steadied. "Yes."

"Then we follow it," he said simply.

She laughed—one small, startled sound that cracked and softened. "You always make it sound so easy."

"It isn't easy," he said. "It's just... what we have to do." His thumb traced the hollow at the base of her throat. "And listen—before the rest of this swallows the day: I'm not going anywhere. I'm with you in this—hotel rooms, courtrooms, whatever comes. You won't look up and find me gone."

The words slid through her like warm tea. The old fear—ridiculous and bone-deep—eased back into its cupboard. She nodded, not trusting her voice.

They unpacked mostly what could be laid flat: a book for the nightstand, her notebook with its small elastic scarred by use, the framed photo of the girls on the steps at Alki, hair backlit to haloes by a low sun. She propped the picture where she could see it from the bed, and for a moment the room held two coasts, the scent of tide and the scent of coal country braided in the steam rising from the radiator.

They FaceTimed home at dusk. The twins' faces bloomed on the screen— Eve with marker on her fingers, Eden already in Maggie's oversize cardigan, sleeves swallowing her wrists. They waved so energetically the image blurred. Stories tumbled out: a spelling test conquered; a soccer ball trapped under the neighbour's Prius; the new cat at the rescue Maggie volunteers with, ear nicked, named Button.

"Are you safe?" Eden asked, face suddenly serious, the way her questions always came from deep inside of her.

"We are," Cassandra said, and meant it more with Owen beside her than she had when alone. "I'm with Dad. We're together. We're okay."

Eve said, "Do the trees look like the trees in your scary books?" then looked faintly scandalized at her own question. "I mean—not the scary part. Just the... moody part."

Cassandra smiled. "They look like paintings trying to remember their colours," she said. "We'll take a picture from the window for you."

Maggie's voice came from somewhere off-screen: *Bedtime, my loves. Kiss your parents through the computer*. They obliged, a pantomime of sweetness that actually reached, somehow, across the country. When the call ended, the room felt larger, then quieter, as if the girls' voices had tightened and tuned the air.

Owen kicked off his shoes and sat on the end of the bed. "Eat with me?" he asked, producing convenience store sandwiches he'd acquired at some juncture.

They ate cross-legged, unwrapping paper that smelled faintly of dill\. They shared a bottle of ginger ale in the hotel's squat tumblers, and he produced, as if by sleight of hand, two napkins that were not the thin, translucent ones from the lobby dispenser but the linen from some forgotten café, probably in the airport terminal. This was his artistry: the dignifying of small things, the refusal to let a day be only what it threatened.

"Tomorrow," he said, "I'll come with you to the house."

She shook her head at once. "It's—" She searched for a word that would hold both danger and futility. "It's a place that wants to make you doubt your own senses. I'd rather not watch it try to work on you."

He considered. "Then I'll wait outside," he said. "On the porch. I'll patch the loose board if I can do it without tools. I'll scare off any ghosts that don't read."

She smiled into the rim of her glass. "They only read the parts where somebody lies and gets away with it."

"Then I'll read them the ending before they're ready." His grin then faded into something gentler. "Whatever you want, Cass. If you want me in the room, I'll be there. If you want to face it alone and see me the minute you're done, I'll be there too."

She reached across the space between them and touched his wrist. "There," she said softly. "Be there."

"Done."

After supper, he drew the heavy curtains and switched on the bedside lamps. Pools of yellow light gathered at their bases, leaving the corners of the room to their mothish shadows. He turned the thermostat down a notch—he always slept best a little cold—and then stretched out beside her, lying on their backs, staring at the stippled ceiling as if someone might have sketched constellations there. The radiator ticked and cooled. Somewhere down the hall a door shut with the weary softness of a long day ending.

"Tell me something good," she said.

He was quiet for a heartbeat, then: "Eden set the table last night without being asked. Forks aligned like soldiers. Eve kissed your picture goodnight and told it not to worry." A breath. "And Mom said to tell you that brave does not mean unafraid. It means in motion anyway. She says she's got the girls until further notice, and she made a list so detailed I'm slightly frightened of it."

"That sounds like her," Cassandra said, warmth pooling at her sternum.

"And something else good," Owen added. "When I landed in Philly, the air smelled the same as it did that first trip we made here, before the girls were born—remember? We traced your old bus route like tourists while you showed me the corners where you learned your way out. I didn't say anything then, but I remember thinking, *We're going to be all right*. And we were. We are."

She turned on her side, propped up on one elbow, and looked at him the way you look at water when you've walked through desert. "Promise me," she said, and the plea had the small, cracked break of childhood in it, embarrassing and true. "Promise me you won't leave—not even in the quiet ways. Not even by pulling back so slowly we both pretend not to notice."

He did not joke, did not deflect. He met the old fear with the steadiness it required. "I promise. I will not abandon you. Not in motion, not in stillness. Not in noise, not in quiet." He lifted her hand, kissed the centre of her palm, then set it back where it had been, as if returning a precious object to its rightful shelf. "If the ground moves—and it will—I'll move with you until it steadies."

The tears came then, not the wrenching kind, but the clean-edges kind that make sight sharper afterward. She let them fall, unhidden. He did not wipe them away; he let them bead and go, as if they, too, had a right to their small paths.

They slept folded into each other, her back to his chest, the inn's old mattress cupping them like a shallow bowl. Sometime near dawn, she woke and lay there listening to the town breathe—the far-off train taking the curve along the river, a plough scraping a side street, a lone car shifting gears on the hill. Beside her, Owen dreamed, breath even, warmth radiating. She thought of the girl in the Whitaker house listening for the sound of a brother's steps, bracing. She thought of the woman now, listening to the same dark for a husband's breath, soft as a vow, and marvelled at the shift in what a night could be asked to hold.

When morning came, it arrived pale and tentative. Owen brought paper cups of coffee from the lobby and a bag of oranges that smelled like a place with proper summers. They stood at the window while the steam rose in ribbons from their cups. Outside, the town performed its incremental awakenings: a bakery light stuttering on, a man in a navy peacoat unlocking a shop door, the river shrugging its mist like a shawl.

"Today," Owen said, "we do one necessary thing and one kind thing."

Cassandra considered. The necessary thing would be a call to the bank, a visit to the clerk, the grinding fact of forms. The kind thing—she thought of Abby's hands, chapped and restless. "Hand lotion," she said. "Unscented. And a soft cardigan that doesn't itch. And new sheets—clean, heavy, soft."

"We'll add a radio," he said. "For good stations on clear days."

She nodded. The list steadied her; it always had. It was not the same as justice, but it was a way to keep human. She took a breath that went all the way down and found not emptiness but a floor.

Owen pressed his cup into her hand, warm palm to warm cardboard. "We go at your pace," he said. "We stop when you say stop. We're not here to prove anything to anyone. We're here because you decided the right thing was still the right thing."

Outside, the mountains hunched closer, and the river kept its own counsel. Inside, in the small square of their room, Cassandra felt the axis tilt the smallest degree toward steadiness. The day would demand too much; the town would offer too little. But she was not alone at the door where she would have to knock, and knock again, and knock after that. She had come to a place that had once been only shadow and learned that even shadow makes space for a hand to find another hand.

"Let's go," she said.

They stepped outside, into the town, into whatever the day would ask— and somewhere beneath all of it, the compass held steady, a quiet needle pointing not to safety, not to certainty, but to the small, stubborn north of truth and doing what is right.

The Unmasking

The following morning, the first headline broke across her laptop screen like glass shattering in her hands.

REKNOWNED HORROR AUTHOR UNMASKED AND EXPLOITING SICK MOTHER

The words burned so bright she almost dropped the device. A photograph accompanied it—grainy, poorly lit, but unmistakable. Cassandra stepping out of the courthouse, papers clutched to her chest, hair whipped across her face by the wind. She looked small, defensive, as though she were already guilty of something unnamed.

Her name was there too. Not Leigh Smith. Not the shield she had built over twenty years of work. The truth, exposed in black type.

CASSANDRA ANDERSON (FORMERLY WHITAKER) UNMASKED AS BESTSELLING HORROR NOVELIST LEIGH SMITH

Her lungs constricted. She read it again and again, until the letters blurred into each other. The secret she had kept so carefully—her separation from Jim Thorpe, her pen name, her work—ripped away by a hand she didn't need to see to recognize.

Darryl. Wendy. Their lawyer.

The articles themselves were venom disguised as narrative. It painted her as a woman who had fled her family, made millions writing about monsters, then returned not with compassion but with greed. Every sentence turned truth on its head. *While her mother wastes away in a crumbling home, Cassandra profits from turning her lies about her family into paperback horror.* The tone was breathless, gleeful, the kind of piece written not to inform but to feed.

She felt the ground tilt.

By evening, the stories metastasized. More and more outlets picked it up. Headlines multiplied, each louder, uglier than the last:

DAUGHTER SEEKS CONTROL OF HOUSE, MONEY

UNMASKED AUTHOR BUILDS EMPIRE ON FAMILY'S BONES

WHITAKER FAMILY BETRAYED FROM WITHIN BY FAMED HORROR WRITER

Her books, once celebrated, became evidence. Pull quotes were yanked out of context, laid alongside Darryl and Wendy's accusations. "Of course she writes horror," one columnist sneered. "She's been rehearsing this since childhood."

On X, the storm rose like fire. Her pen name—her sanctuary—was trending.

Leigh Smith is Cassandra Whitaker. Remember that.
Burn the bitch 🐍
She feeds on pain and lies. Even her mother's.

The snake emoji slithered endlessly through the feed, a digital hiss. It coiled under her author photographs, across her book covers, beneath fan art she had once saved with quiet gratitude. Her readers turned into a mob, or perhaps they had never truly been hers. Each insult was a strike, a lash, another layer of skin peeled away.

She shut her laptop, but it didn't stop. The words had already crawled inside her skull, branding themselves against her ribs. She felt them under her skin, searing, a fever she could not sweat out.

Owen awoke to find her sitting on the hotel bed, posture stiff, eyes hollow.

"Cass?" He turned to her. His voice was steady, but his hands reached for her as if she might vanish.

She opened her laptop and turned it to him. He scrolled, his jaw tightening, his breath sharp through his nose. She watched him read, his face shadowed by the blue light, until finally he looked up.

"They've outed you as Leigh Smith." His words were quiet, heavy.

Cassandra nodded once. "Everything I built—Leigh Smith—it's gone. They've gutted it in a day."

Owen sat up beside her, pulling her into the curve of his body. His warmth anchored her, but she couldn't stop trembling. She felt like the hotel walls themselves were listening, like the entire town pressed its ear to the door.

That night, she tried to sleep, but the mob invaded even her dreams. She stood on a stage, spotlighted, while faceless figures in the crowd chanted in unison: *Burn the bitch. Burn the bitch.* Their voices grew louder until the sound rattled her teeth. She woke gasping, her throat raw, as though she had been screaming with them.

In the morning, the phone began to ring. Publishers. Agents. Publicists. Panic laced every call. "We need to draft a statement." "We need to control the narrative." "We can't let this spiral."

But it had already spiraled.

She sat at the small desk in the hotel room, laptop open, cursor blinking. The tide outside roared faintly, muffled by the mountains, but she could not feel its steadiness. Her hands hovered over the keys, then began to type.

My name is Cassandra Anderson. It used to be Cassandra Whitaker. Many of you know me as Leigh Smith. I began writing under a pen name because I wanted my work to stand apart from the shadows of my life. The stories I told came from the deepest parts of me, yes, but they were never about exploitation–they were about survival. I came to Jim Thorpe not for profit, but to care for a mother who can no longer care for herself. I understand not everyone will believe me. But I will continue to do what I believe is right, even when it costs me.

She read it twice. Her throat closed. Then she hit send.

Within minutes it her publicist had posted it. Almost immediately, ridicule poured back like acid.

Of course she's spinning it. What a liar.
Survival? Please. She's feeding on her mom like one of her monsters.
Snake 🐍 Burn the bitch.

Her publicist called again, voice tight. "It's not helping. They're doubling down."

Cassandra closed her laptop. She couldn't bear to look anymore. Her reflection stared back from the black glass: pale, hollow-eyed, hair falling loose. A woman dissolving under the weight of a thousand strangers' hate.

Owen touched her shoulder. "They can destroy the name," he said softly. "But they can't destroy you."

She turned toward him, eyes burning. "Can't they? They've taken everything we've built. They've turned it into proof that I'm a monster."

He pulled her close, pressing his forehead to hers. "You're not a monster. You're the woman who stayed up all night editing a school project with Eve until she stopped crying. You're the mother who taught Eden how to hold her fear in her palm and name it. You're the woman who sacrificed her own peace for a mother who definitely does not deserve your efforts. They can't erase that. Not ever."

His certainty steadied her for a breath, but when she lay down, the chant returned. Burn the bitch. Burn the bitch. The chorus of a world that had decided truth was too quiet to hear.

The compass inside her trembled. For the first time, she wondered if it had been pointing her wrong all along.

The Statement That Fell Silent

The statement arrived in Cassandra's inbox just before dawn, a draft her publicist had stayed up all night polishing. The email subject line read simply: *For Immediate Release.*

She clicked it open with hands that trembled, though not from coffee.

"Cassandra Whitaker, known to readers as Leigh Smith, has always lived privately. She returned to Pennsylvania not for publicity, but to care for her mother in her time of need. Allegations made against her are categorically false. She will continue to put her family's wellbeing before all else."

The words were neat, sterile, polished into corporate rhythm. They sat on the screen like a glass wall—transparent, clean, but cold.

Cassandra read it once, then again. Her chest ached. The statement was true, in its way, but stripped of her voice, it sounded hollow. It reduced her story to a handful of sentences, all the raw edges sanded down. The compass in her chest twisted uneasily.

Her publicist's follow-up pinged a moment later: *It's the best we can do. We have to keep it simple. The more emotional we get, the easier it is for them to tear apart. We'll circulate to the trades, then to the big sites. Brace yourself.*

Brace yourself.

She closed the laptop and stared at the ceiling of the hotel room, where light from the streetlamp painted watery gold across the plaster. Beside her, Owen still slept, one arm flung across the sheet, his breath slow and steady. She wanted to crawl into that rhythm, to let it carry her like tide. But the words burned on her screen, demanding release.

At nine a.m., the statement went live.

By ten, the ridicule began.

"She'll continue to put her family's wellbeing before all else." Sure, Jan.
A horror writer caring for her mom? Sounds like research for the next book.
Categorically false? This Karen is categorically full of shit.

Memes sprouted like mould. A photo of Cassandra outside the courthouse, eyes downcast, turned into a looping gif with captions: *When Mom says she needs soup but you're busy cashing her cheques.* Her book covers were photoshopped—snakes slithering across the titles, flames licking the edges, her author photo warped into a sneer.

The phrase *family's wellbeing* became a punchline. Users paired it with pictures of empty fridges, broken-down houses, even horror-movie stills of daughters standing over dead mothers. The cruelty was relentless, inventive, viral.

By noon, Cassandra's phone buzzed without pause. Mentions poured in by the thousands, each one a fresh lash. The snake emoji hissed across her screen, accompanied now by fire, by skulls, by knives.

Burn the bitch 🐍🔥
"Well-being" = $$$
Leigh Smith = Cassandra Whitaker = parasite.

She set her phone face down on the table, but the silence was worse. She could feel the noise vibrating through the screen, as though the world outside the window had turned against her, pressing closer, hungrier.

Her body betrayed her. Hands shaking. Pulse racing. Breath shallow. She pressed her palms flat against her thighs, willing herself to be still, but the tremors carried on. She hadn't felt this powerless since she was a child in the Whitaker house, waiting for footsteps to pad across her room. The mob outside was faceless, but it was the same cruelty, magnified—this time with an audience cheering it on.

Owen, freshly showered, found her at the desk, staring at the back of her phone.

"They don't believe me," she whispered.

He crouched beside her. His hand cupped the back of her neck, grounding her. "You don't need them to believe you. You only need to keep standing."

Her throat closed. "But standing against what? Lies spread faster than anything. They'll ruin every part of me."

He kissed her temple. "They can ruin you. They can't ruin the truth. And they can't ruin us."

But when night came, and she scrolled against her better judgment, the truth felt like a small candle flickering against a hurricane.

Someone had clipped her statement and set it to ominous music, overlaying photos of her books, her face, her mother's house, the courthouse steps. The video ended with one final line in dripping red font: *She says she'll put family first. Her family says otherwise.*

It had over a million views.

The comments beneath swelled into a bonfire culminating in a video of a chanting crowd surrounding a fire fed with the pages of her novels.

Liar. Snake. Monster. Burn. Burn. Burn.

She closed the laptop so hard it rattled the desk lamp.

In the silence after, the chant still roared in her head, the way thunder lingers after lightning is gone. She pressed her hands to her ears, but there was no shutting it out. The mob had crawled inside her.

And the statement, meant to shield her, had fallen silent.

The Hollowing Out

It began with a single email.

The subject line was as sharp and bloodless as a scalpel: *Contract Update.*

Cassandra opened it with the casual dread of a woman who already knew bad news when she saw it. The words inside were worse than expected—polite, distant, irrevocable. *We've decided to postpone publication indefinitely.* The publisher thanked her for her "hard work," praised her "extraordinary vision," and slid the knife in with a single phrase: *Given recent publicity, we believe this is the best course of action for both parties.*

Both parties.

As though her life, gutted and dragged through the streets, was a mutual arrangement.

She stared at the email until her coffee went cold. Then another message arrived, this one from a literary magazine that had begged for her words only months before. We've decided to go in a different direction. *Another from a podcast host: In light of recent revelations, we'll be cancelling our interview.* And then the silence, heavier than any email. Agents who once called weekly stopped returning messages. Editors who used to gush about her "voice" and "vision" vanished into static.

Her career didn't collapse all at once. It withered, petal by petal, until all that remained was a stalk of memory stripped bare.

At the same time, Darryl and Wendy sharpened their performance. They had learned quickly how to weaponize the system, how to use the machinery of law and order as a theatre stage.

It began with phone calls to the police. *She yelled at Abby*, they said. *She shoved her*. Then came claims that Cassandra was stealing—purses rifled, money missing, jewellery pocketed. Each lie was absurd, easily disproved, but that was never the point. Every call forced officers to knock on the sagging door of the inn, to log a report, to look at Cassandra with suspicion already inked into their notebooks.

And then came Darrly and Wendy's escalation. Harassment, they said. Social media abuse. Cassandra laughed bitterly when she first heard it— her accounts had been dormant for months, her publicist too afraid to touch them. But the police didn't laugh. They came anyway. Every accusation became a line on a report, another nail in the coffin of her credibility.

The worst part wasn't the lies themselves. It was the repetition, the attrition. Each visit was a reminder that truth carried no weight here. Each shrug from an officer was another ounce of herself chipped away.

The final visit broke something in her.

Brady, the police officer she trusted—the one who had told her about the assault, who had seemed to believe her—took her aside after Wendy's latest performance, her voice shrill with fabricated outrage. His eyes were tired, his cap tucked under one arm.

"Look," he said quietly. "I know what's happening. I know they're using the system to wear you down. But there's nothing we can do. Every call has to be answered. Every allegation has to be logged. And every time, it chips away at you. That's the design. They know it."

Her throat tightened. "So I'm just supposed to let them? Let them keep lying, keep dragging me through this?"

His mouth pressed into a grim line. "My advice?" He hesitated, then sighed. "Withdraw. Walk away. Before there's nothing left of you."

Cassandra stood frozen, the air sharp in her lungs. Walk away. As if walking away hadn't been the crime she'd been accused of her entire life. As if abandoning her mother now wouldn't be twisted into proof of her cruelty. But beneath her fury was exhaustion so deep it hollowed her out from the inside, marrow scraped clean.

That night, she and Owen packed their suitcases.

The house smelled of mould and rot, urine soaked into carpet, smoke ground into wallpaper. Abby sat in her chair, muttering nonsense—scrambled eggs, bus tickets, the roof won't stay put. Cassandra bent and kissed her mother's temple. The skin was papery, cool, the texture of withered petals. She whispered, "I tried." Whether Abby heard or not, she couldn't tell.

When she closed the door, it felt like the house exhaled, relieved to see her go.

Back in Seattle, the ocean was still there. The gulls still wheeled above Alki Point, the tide still rose and fell. Owen was waiting at the airport, the girls running into her arms, their warmth fierce enough to nearly break her.

But she carried emptiness inside her, a hollowness that no embrace could fill.

Her writing room was unchanged. Shelves of books stared down at her—classics she had hunted for, first editions she had once cradled like relics, her own novels lined in neat succession. But they no longer looked like triumphs. They looked like gravestones. Her pen name—Leigh Smith—had become a carcass picked clean by strangers' hands.

The phone still rang with numbers she didn't recognize. Sometimes she picked up, and silence lingered before a click. Sometimes it was a voice hissing: Burn the bitch. More often it was nothing at all, but even silence had become a weapon now.

At night, she lay awake listening to the sea. The sound had once steadied her, each wave a reminder of persistence. Now it seemed to echo her own emptiness: endless, restless, hollow.

One evening, she sat in her office with the lights off, only the window glowing faintly with reflected city light. Her reflection stared back—gaunt, eyes shadowed, hair unkempt. She lifted a hand to the glass, her palm cold against the pane. She imagined the mob on the other side, faces pressed close, breath fogging the glass, waiting for her to slip.

Owen came in quietly, his presence filling the room with warmth she couldn't feel. He knelt beside her chair, rested his head against her knee. He didn't speak. He didn't need to.

She tangled her fingers in his hair, held tight, and whispered, "They've taken everything."

"No," he said softly. "Not everything. Not us. Not them." He tilted his head toward the sound of the twins' laughter echoing faintly down the hall. "That's ours. That can't be hollowed out."

But Cassandra knew better. The compass inside her no longer pointed anywhere. It spun wildly, useless, as if mocking her belief that the right thing had been worth following.

And for the first time in her life, she wasn't sure if there was any way back.

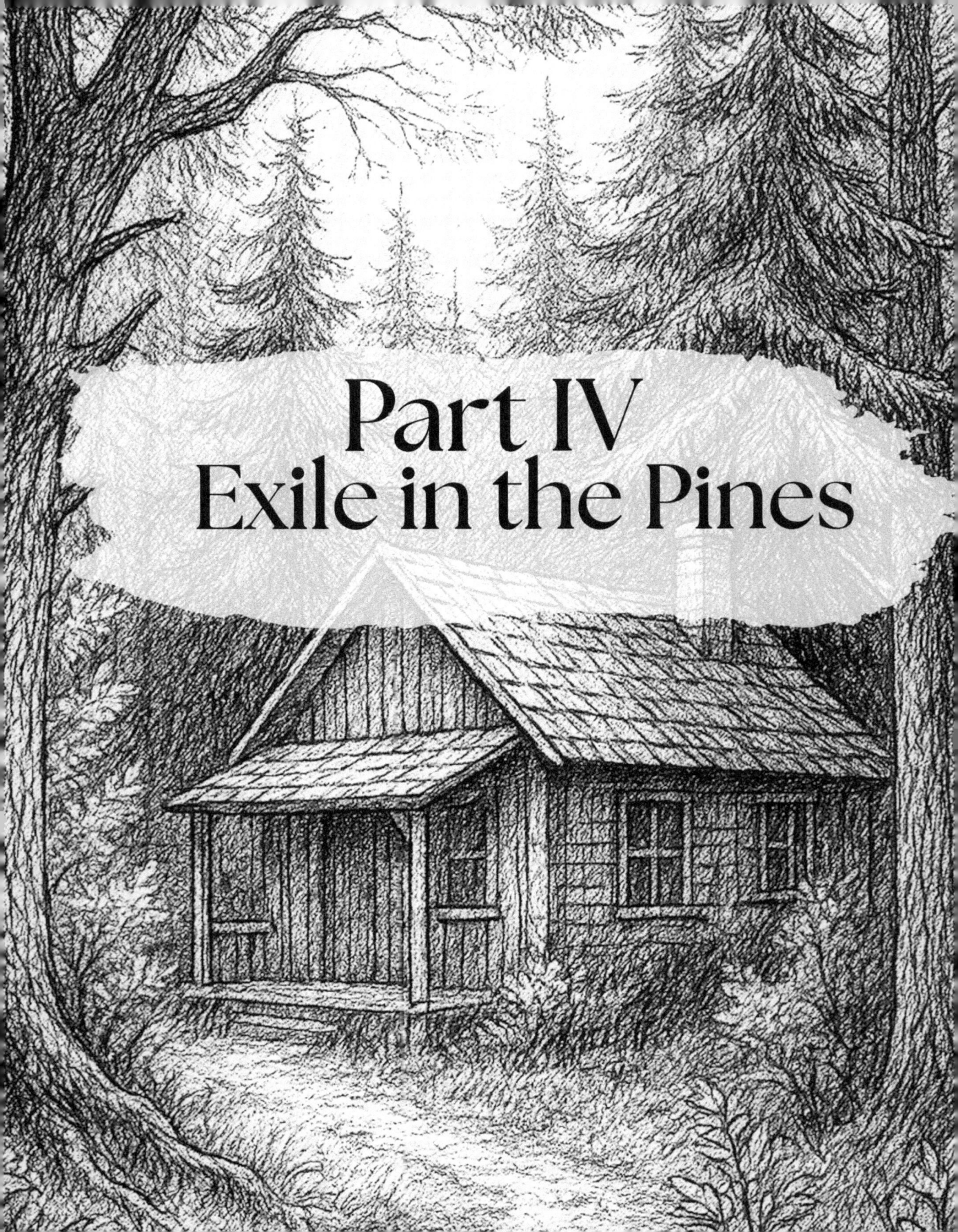

Part IV
Exile in the Pines

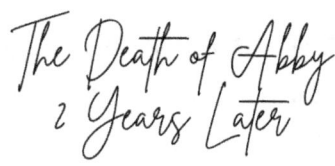

The Death of Abby
2 Years Later

Two years folded over themselves like the damp pages of a paperback left out in the rain. Time, in Seattle, arranged itself around small rituals—Eve's saxophone practice dissolving into laughter, Eden's habit of labelling the spice jars in a tidy, looping hand, Owen's evening soups that tasted the way memory feels when it's kind. Cassandra learned to live inside the smaller compass of ordinary days. The ocean breathed. The twins kept growing. Words returned to her in hesitant drifts that she did not force into books. The world narrowed to a shape she could hold.

And then the phone rang.

She was shelling peas at the kitchen island, the window flung open on a pewter afternoon, the Sound choppy and slate-coloured beyond the glass. The number was unfamiliar, but something in her bones knew, even before she swiped to answer.

"Cass." Darryl's voice had not changed so much as calcified—less a voice than a scrape. "Mom's dead."

The peas rolled from her hand, pattering across the cutting board like small green marbles.

"Repeat that," she said. She could hear her own caution, the way one speaks to a stranger at the door.

"She died." He sounded almost bored. Then, as if remembering the performance, he added, "Last night. Or the night before. The nurse said—

whatever. She's gone." A pause, not for grief, but for effect. "There's going to be a funeral. Costs and whatnot. I can't pay. She's got nothing. So if you want anything done about it, you're up."

Owen had turned from the kitchen sink, dish towel in his hands, the kind of quiet he wore when something mattered. She met his eyes over the phone in her hand; he crossed to the counter and, without a word, set his own phone down beside hers, opened the voice memo app, and pressed record.

"What happened?" Cassandra asked, though what she meant was *how did it end*—and also *how did it begin*, as if he might be able to name the moment in that collapsing house when a woman's edges came finally apart.

"Old age or whatever." A snort. "You know. Head was gone ages ago. She didn't have money for the home. They've been on me to pay, and I'm not getting stuck with that. So they said they're calling you, but I figured I'd—" he chose the word with a kind of false tenderness that turned her stomach "—loop you in."

Loop you in.

"What home?" she said. Her voice was very calm. The calm she'd learned as a child when calmness was the only door that ever opened.

"Long-term care," he said. "You'd know that if you hadn't run away." Then, before she could answer, he continued, impatient, transactional. "Here's the thing. The county's going to want to release the body. But if there's no payment, they'll let the state take care of it. Cremation, no service, all that. Unless you want to step up and put a card down."

There it was: the bill, dressed like a choice. Grief stapled to an invoice.

"Where is she?" Cassandra asked.

"Mortuary." He named a place she dimly recognised, down by the river, a brick building whose windows she had once walked past without looking in. "They're holding her, for now. But they'll release if nobody pays. So." He let the word hang, as if generosity might gather around it of its own accord. "Clock's ticking."

She closed her eyes and saw the last time: the papery skin of Abby's temple, the way her breath had come in ragged, unmeaningful phrases—*scrambled eggs, bus tickets, the roof won't stay put*. Cassandra had whispered I tried into the fragile cup of her ear. Whether it had landed anywhere was a mystery. A child's message tucked into a bottle and thrown to sea.

"I'm sorry she died," Cassandra said. It felt like putting a stone where a stone belonged. "I hope, at the end, someone was kind."

Darryl chuckled. "She didn't know what was happening. Didn't matter."

Silence opened between them, a dark river.

Then his voice changed. It went soft; he shifted, as she had always known he would, from demand to something he liked to think of as charm. "Listen, Cass. We could do this together, you and me. If you just—help out, you know? Cover the costs, organise the service. People should say goodbye."

She could hear the splintering of the floor under that sentence, the trap door hidden in it. "No," she said. "I won't pay you to perform grief."

He exhaled through his nose, theatrically wounded. "Wow. Cold. Figures. You never were family."

The word hit her where he meant it to. Family. As if the thing he had been given and she had been denied was an inheritance she should regret not cherishing. She set the knife down, the blade bright with the green sheen of peas, and looked out at the water until her trachea loosened.

"Darryl," she said, "did you threaten to let the state dispose of your mother's body if I didn't pay you?"

There was a little flick—fear? calculation?—in the pause that followed. "It's not like that."

"How is it like?"

"It's like—there's no money and somebody has to handle it and I'm not—" He broke off. The tone hardened. "You think you're clever, don't you? With your—" the word curdled "—books. You think you can make me say something that sounds bad when you write it down."

"You do that yourself," she said softly.

Something snapped. The performance peeled away; what stood in its place was older, meaner, truer. "You listen to me," he hissed. "You're not safe. You think you are, with your view and your fancy house. But I know where you live. I know where you are. I know him, and I know your bitch daughters."

Owen's hands tightened around the stone countertop.

Darryl continued, fast now, breathless with the pleasure of saying the unsayable. He named their street. Their city. He spoke the twins' names into the receiver—Eve first, then Eden—as if rolling hard candy on his tongue. "Pretty girls," he said. "Shame if anything happened. Shame if they had to find out what kind of person their mother really is."

Cassandra's vision narrowed, then brightened with a kind of cold, lucid light. Owen had shifted closer; one of his hands moved to the small of her back, the weight of it an iron, grounding her into the floor.

"Stop," she said. "Stop now."

"Or what?" he said. "You'll cry to the cops? People just say things, remember? That's what they told you, right? So what. I can say whatever I want. Free country."

He said the new pen name, too—the one Cassandra had chosen like a fresh shirt pulled over a scar. He said it as if it were a secret he had wrestled to the ground himself. "How's the romance gig, Cassy Wolf?" he jeered. "Cute. Real cute."

"How did you get that?" Cassandra asked. Her voice was level, but there was a sheen on everything now, the world slicked with unreality.

"People talk," he sang. "People sell. Internet tells you what you want to know if you know what to ask. Wendy's cousin works at a place that—

never mind. Point is, I know it. I know you. You can't hide."

He kept going, the way men do when they've found a rhythm that tastes like power: a litany of places they might show up, a catalogue of harms dressed as hypotheticals. Her mailbox. The girls' school. Owen's mother's address. The new post office box attached to the pen name. Each fact was a small burn laid onto her skin.

Owen remained steady at her side.

Cassandra pressed her fingers against the counter to keep them from shaking. She looked at the knife. At the peas. At the water beyond the window, steady and indifferent, as it had been the day she was born and the day her father died and every day since.

"Darryl," she said, very quietly, "you are threatening my children."

He laughed. "I'm just talking. People just say things, remember?"

She hung up.

The kitchen became a bell she had been struck inside. Sound went on ringing. She did not notice she had been holding her breath until Owen's palm found the back of her neck and warmth moved through her like a dispensation.

"Everything's recorded," he said. His voice was the sound a harbour makes when fog closes and a ship finds it anyway. "Everything."

She nodded. "Call," she said. The word was threadbare, but it held. She meant the police. She meant *now*.

They came. Two officers in dark blue, badges shining too brightly in the soft kitchen light. The younger one clicked his pen and took notes in a little book, writing as if the speed of his scribbling might serve as evidence of care. The older man—thick around the middle, wedding band dulled by decades of plumbing soap—leaned against the doorway in that careful way that says we are listening but also we have already half-decided.

Owen queued the recording and pressed play. Darryl's voice filled their kitchen—greasy, familiar, undeniable. He named the girls; he named the street; he curled his mouth around the new pen name with the satisfaction of a thief who has finally found the seam. When it ended, the younger officer looked up and glanced at the older one with something that might have been unease.

"Well," the older man said, clearing his throat. "That's... not good to hear."

"It's a threat," Cassandra said. She could hear the steadiness in her own voice and was grateful for it as though for a borrowed coat. "Against minors. He named them. He named our address."

The older man lifted a shoulder. "People say things when they're upset."

"Sir," Owen said, and there was iron under his courtesy, "he did not express sorrow. He weaponised information. He threatened our children."

The officer's gaze slid to the ocean beyond the window, as if the answer might be out there, riding a freighter into the bay. Then he sighed. "Here's the thing. He didn't say he was going to do anything. He didn't give a specific plan or timeline. We can take a report"—he gestured at the younger man's wrist, already moving—"and we can flag your address for patrols for a bit. But it's a civil issue unless he shows up or does something actionable. My advice?" He paused, as if conferring a favour. "If you're worried, move. Change your numbers. Maybe consider changing that pen name again if it's already out there."

Cassandra stared at him. There was a moment in which she felt she might laugh; the laugh would be a bright, brittle sound, a glass dropped from a great height. "Move," she said. "Change our life? Again?"

"It's not fair," the younger officer blurted, then flushed, as if he had embarrassed himself by letting truth slip. "But—" He looked to his partner for the rest of the sentence; the rest of the sentence never came.

The older man nodded once to signal the close of something that had never properly opened. "You folks take care now."

After they left, the kitchen felt larger and emptier, the way rooms do when a party ends and everyone goes home without saying goodbye. The peas lay in a small green scatter on the counter, the knife shining a line of light like a thin idea of mercy.

Cassandra sank onto a stool. The ocean kept breathing. On the fridge, the twins' school pictures grinned with gap-toothed bravado, as if they could hold back anything with the force of their joy.

Owen came to stand between her knees, his hands on her shoulders. He did not say *we'll be all right*, because he would not cheapen either of them that way. He said, "We'll do the next necessary thing."

"What is it?" she asked, because sometimes being told what to do was a relief, an abdication offered by love and accepted as a strategy.

"We call your mother's mortuary ourselves," he said. "We refuse to let him be the only voice in the room. We find out what dignity looks like that we can afford."

"And then?"

"Then we make a plan to leave." He swallowed. "I know the officer's suggestion was an insult dressed as advice. But he wasn't wrong about the physics. If the ground moves under you, sometimes you step off it."

She nodded. The body has ways of agreeing before the heart catches up.

They called. The woman at the mortuary had a voice like old hymnals—thin with use, steady with custom. She confirmed the fact. Abby had died. She described the options and the prices with a compassion that kept a shameful enterprise from becoming pure humiliation. Cassandra chose the least awful path and gave her card number with the abstracted dignity of a person paying for a stranger's coat in a shop window.

After, she stood at the sink and washed her hands though they were not dirty. The twins tiptoed in, solemn with that particular childhood intuition that recognises the weather in a room. Eve pressed a paper heart she had cut from construction paper into Cassandra's palm. Eden stood guard at the window as if daring the horizon to be anything other than faithful sea.

"How do we keep safe?" Eden asked, whittled down to the bone of the question.

"Abigail Whitaker," Cassandra said. The syllables felt like stones, and it was a relief to put them down.

"Say ours," he said.

"Eve," she said. "Eden." A breath. "Owen." She placed her own last, as if that might once and for all make room. "Cassandra."

Owen reached for her hand and threaded his fingers through. "We make the leaving an act of protection," he said. "Not surrender. We will not be chased. We will choose."

In the window, their reflection looked like a small, stubborn votive against the dark—two figures, two handprints on the glass where earlier the officers had looked out as if truth might be docked offshore. The ocean kept breathing, unconcerned with human reliquaries, unfazed by names. The night did not close like a door; it opened like a field.

"Tomorrow," she said, and the word did not tremble. "We begin."

Exile in the Pines

They left on a weekday because weekdays seemed less conspicuous. Dawn still had its hand on the city when they loaded the last boxes; the gulls were only beginning to rake their cries across the pale sky. Owen checked the latches twice, then a third time, while Cassandra stood in the doorway of her writing room and looked at what was no longer hers. The shelves had been stripped to their bones. Sun rectangles paled the wall where frames had hung—ghosts of squares and rectangles, a geometry of departure. The built-in desk, bare and innocent, showed the nicks where a life had been sharpened.

Eve and Eden pressed their palms to the windows as they pulled away from the curb. The house held steady until the corner, then slid out of view, a photograph returning to its envelope.

They crossed the mountains in weather that couldn't make up its mind. One pass wrapped the highway in fog; another opened the sky as if a hand had lifted, pouring blue across the windshield. The border guard asked polite questions in a voice that suggested he had already heard every story a human could tell. When he said, "Welcome home," to Owen, Cassandra felt the sentence snag in her ribs. Home, she repeated to herself—not as statement but as instruction.

The Columbia Valley unspooled like a hidden corridor. Radium Hot Springs sat in its crumple of stone and light, the highway threading through a gate of rock as if the mountains had split their ribs to let them in. Bighorn sheep grazed the verge with the indifference of animals who know the land belongs to them. The air carried the faint sulphur of the springs, metallic and ancient, as though the earth itself were breathing through a cracked tooth.

The property was an off-grid parcel on a lopsided slope of lodgepole pine and spruce, twenty minutes from town if the track behaved, forty if it didn't. Owen had found it through a friend's friend who'd said, *It's rough but honest; it won't ask for anything you can't give.* A small cabin, two outbuildings, a slant-roofed shed sagging under last winter's memory. Solar panels settled into the clearing like dark water. A blue plastic barrel caught rain off the metal eaves. The well head crouched in a circle of rocks, lid bolted tight. Beyond, a ridge shouldered up into the sky, stitched with cutlines and deer trail.

"Listen," Owen said. The children stopped moving. Cassandra did too. The silence was not silence; it was a thick braid of small sounds. A wind combing needles. The tentative tap of a nuthatch. The far-off shush of river. She felt her shoulders climb toward her ears and then—oddly—fall. The city's constant hum had been a cloth pressed over her face; this quiet was a new kind of fabric, coarser, breathable.

Inside, the cabin smelled of soft rot and old woodstove, the ghosts of a dozen winters. Mouse droppings on the sill suggested the housekeeping had been informal. Owen opened windows; Eden swept with missionary zeal; Eve began naming spiders as if baptism conferred tenancy. Cassandra stood in the doorway and let the mountain air push past her, a cool hand on a fevered brow.

They worked until light tipped. As with all first days in strange places, tasks became decisions, decisions became arguments, arguments became small apologies, and finally the work turned into the kind of weariness that says bed is not a place but an answer. They unrolled sleeping bags on mattresses that had been left behind and pretended not to mind. In the middle of the night, an owl called in a voice older than language.

Cassandra woke with a start—heart galloping, palms clammy—then lay there and counted her daughters' breaths across the dark.

It took three days to build a rhythm and three weeks to learn it was not rhythm at all but attention. Off-grid meant listening. To the sun's angle, since it powered their lights and their patience. To the forecast, because a forgotten cloud could become a day surrendered to mist. To the woodpile's height. To the generator's mood. To the way water moved in the hose when the pump had had enough and needed rest. To the oven that was not an oven but a box that sometimes consented to heat.

Mornings: Owen started the stove and it argued with flame before acquiescing; the kettle wheezed toward boil; the girls called from the loft that today they would be alpine explorers or pioneers of radical domesticity. Cass warmed her hands around a mug that steamed like thought. She watched a chipmunk choose between caution and greed along the railing and felt a kinship too sharp to be charming.

Afternoons: the valley's light came at an angle that made even ordinary branches look like brushstrokes. On days when the clouds sealed the bowl of the sky, the clearing kept its own dim weather. Eve practised scales on a thrift-store keyboard the panels could barely forgive; Eden did math with a pencil she sharpened too often because precision was the only relief she knew.
School, such as it was, became a table with books and a parent's dignity tied like a ribbon to the attempt.

Nights: the dark here had a body. It leaned against the roof and listened. They learned each sound by heart—the creak of an old board, the skip of something small across the porch, the far bark of a neighbour's dog that lived two clearings away and was thus practically kin. When the sky was clean it carried a cold thick with stars. The twins lay on the steps with their heads close and tried to name constellations; Cassandra could not help them. Her old cities had had other maps.

She did not write.

At first, not-writing felt like a holiday she had earned. She stacked wood. She learned the generator's choke like a prayer. She found her hands memorising the tight twist that made the clothesline true. Each domestic success skimmed a small, clear satisfaction from the day. When time tried to open for her—when the girls were reading and Owen was mending the shed door and the light fell across the table like a page—she felt the old instinct rise. Then she put it down gently, as if it were a bird that would only harm itself flinging against the glass.

After a week, not-writing became a discipline, then a penance, then— without her noticing—an identity. She stopped carrying a notebook. The old reflex of reaching for a line when a sentence offered itself in the trees, in the shape of the ridge or the gesture of a cloud, became a reprimand. She looked away. She told herself she was resisting the impulse to narrate her survival. She told herself silence was her offering to the girls, to Owen, to the clearings, to a life that had asked for too many explanations and too much proof. She told herself that telling the truth had cost her everything; now she would keep it and spend it nowhere.

Owen did not press. That was his genius and his flaw; he would hold a line until it went slack or steady of its own accord. He split wood with grave attention. He kept lists in a small notebook that had nothing in it but measurements and parts numbers and the unglamorous arithmetic of getting through a winter. His hands, which had once passed over blueprints and baby scalps with the same reverence, became instruments of maintenance. Acts of love, every one.

He drove to town on Thursdays for supplies and mail. Sometimes he came back with nothing addressed to them; sometimes there was a letter in a stranger's hand that began, Dear Leigh— and ended with the awkward, unkillable gratitude of a reader who had been altered by a book. The first time, he laid it gently on the table beside her tea, a small thing offered like a found feather. Cassandra covered it with her palm for a moment as if warming something wounded, then pushed it back.

"Not now," she said.

He nodded and tucked it into a drawer.

Maggie came once a month, arriving from the Island in a small car that wore road dust like pride. She brought sourdough in tea towels and stories the twins devoured—the cat at the hospice who slept only on quilts; the boy at the store who mistook thyme for mint and ruined his grandmother's tea. She never asked Cassandra about writing. She asked her about the pump. About how the stove drew in crosswind. About whether the girls liked the new brand of cocoa. It was a mercy so exact Cassandra sometimes had to step outside to breathe it.

Late autumn leaned into winter without asking permission. Snow came in a polite dusting and then, all at once, a certainty. The cabin took on its winter posture—shoulders hunched, snowcap dignified. The world slimmed to the track down to the road and the path between the door and the woodpile. The twins learned the sound of new snow under boots, the tiny, jubilant squeak when the cold deepened and the air itself seemed to grow glassy. One afternoon a herd of elk threaded the treeline like a thought returning; the girls went still, as if sound could break a spell. A cow looked back with a gaze so steady Eden cried.

The mountains did not care who they sheltered. That indifference was its own mercy. On nights that layered wind upon wind and set the trees to talking in their own ruined Latin, the cabin became a held breath. Owen moved through the rooms with lantern light, checking latches, tucking blankets, conferring his quiet on each bed. Cassandra lay awake and listened to the snow shift its weight on the roof, a gradual settle like a patient choosing a better position.

Sometimes, after the girls fell asleep, she took a book down and held it without opening. Her own spine on the shelf beside strangers looked like a cousin at a funeral—a face you know but do not want to meet at the buffet. Once, in an unguarded hour, she opened to a random page of *The Shadows of Ashfield*, that first manuscript long since reborn as a book with a cover that now felt like a dare. She read a paragraph and then another. The sentences were knives she had forged and she could not decide whether to admire them or throw them into the snow. She closed the book and slid it back until the shelf swallowed it.

Eve and Eden adjusted the way children do: fully in the day, and then later, in secret cracks, not at all. Eve found a tree she named Cathedral and read at its base until her legs went numb. Eden kept a ledger of small observations—the pattern of a woodpecker's holes, the hour the ridge first caught light, the difference between a moose track and a man's. In the evenings they learned cribbage from Maggie and counted victories in beans. They missed their friends with an ache they tried to hide and sometimes failed. On those nights, Cassandra lay between them and listened to them breathe, then fell asleep with her face tilted toward the ceiling as if listening for a line that would not come.

In February, smoke from far-off fires drifted an hour before dawn and left the sky the colour of a bruise all day. It was wrong smoke—out-of-season, metallic, threaded with a dread that outlasted it. Cassandra stood on the porch with her hand on the rail and thought, *Even the air has started lying*. She went inside and scrubbed the kettle although it was clean.

Spring loosened winter like a knot worked by patient fingers. The first rain on metal became a drum she had forgotten she loved. Small things revealed themselves: a hard green knuckle on a branch, a vole's sudden braid across a path, the mountain opening one more shade of blue. The twins began to forget the particular fear of stepping into boots cold from a porch; they screamed once and laughed after.

Cassandra planted herbs in a trough and could not keep the basil from bolting. She let it go. She had no appetite for disciplining anything that wanted to run toward seed.

Visitors from town arrived the way weather did: suddenly, and with their own climate. A neighbour named Ruth brought a pie and scolded Owen for not covering the woodpile. "You'll pay twice for every stick you don't keep dry," she said, in a voice that was not unkind. A man with a chainsaw for a laugh offered to plough their track "for a friendly rate," which meant more than they wanted to pay and less than he wanted to charge. They learned the choreography: what to say, where to stop. They learned every face had a cousin in another story.

In all of it, Cassandra's silence grew into its own room. At night, when Owen slept with his hand open so that she could fit hers into it without waking him, she stared at the ceiling and measured the distance between self-preservation and erasure. She had chosen not to write because the world had mistaken her truth for appetite and she could not bear to give the world one more bite. But the not-writing began to feel less like defence and more like drift. Her mind, once a precise instrument, dulled to domestic edges: how many logs until midnight, how much sun in the battery bank, whether the sky's paler patch meant rain or mercy.

On a bright morning in May, a letter arrived addressed to Cassy Wolf at the post office box they checked every Tuesday. No return address, just a familiar slope-shouldered hand. Owen brought it back, placed it on the table, and watched her the way one watches someone approach a river they've sworn not to cross.

Cassandra stood for a long time. The girls looked from the letter to her, then found the surface of the table intensely interesting in a way that was its own form of prayer. She picked it up finally, turned it over, and set it down again.

Not now, she meant to say. But the words that came were, "Later."

That night she burned the envelope in the woodstove with the rest of the day's newsprint. She watched it curl and blacken, watched the flame take the paper's shape and then its absence. The cabin's small window caught the flicker and returned it as a weak star.

"Does it help?" Owen asked.

"It doesn't hurt," she said.

He nodded.

Summer crept in and the creek near the bottom of the slope unbuttoned itself. The twins waded in water so cold it turned their legs a comic-book pink. They collected stones and gave them names. They began to understand that happiness in exile is not contradiction but craft, an arrangement of small glories into something almost like a day.

On a Sunday, Cassandra walked the cutline to the ridge alone. A hawk unstitched the sky above her. She sat on a fallen trunk and took inventory. Fingers, capable. Chest, tight but not locked. Mind, a room with less furniture than before but still a window that opened. She did not reach for a pen. She looked at the place where a sentence might have been and counted to sixty.

A wind came up from the valley and moved through the tops of the pines with a sound like pages turning. She laughed at the cruelty of it, and then—because she could not help it—at the beauty. She put her face in her hands and let both sounds happen in the same mouth.

When she walked back, the cabin came into view the way cabins do when someone loves you from inside them—the smoke straighter, the door slightly ajar, a figure at the edge of the clearing shading his eyes to find you at the point where trail becomes yard. She lifted a hand. Owen lifted his. The girls burst from behind him like ungainly birds, shouting about a moth the size of a saucer and a pie that had failed and would someone come witness its failure before it cooled.

Cassandra stepped across the threshold and the house accepted her, as if each time she returned it recalculated the size it needed to be to hold this version of her. She thought: *Silence is what I have. Silence is what keeps us. Silence is how we breathe here.* She did not know if it was wisdom or cowardice; she did not try to name it. Naming had cost her too much.

After supper, she stood at the sink and watched the dusk remove the last colour from the ridge. The girls quarrelled softly about whose turn it was to take the compost and ended up going together, because this was the year they had learned that companionship is not a prize but a technique. Owen leaned in the doorway and said nothing and said everything.

She wiped her hands, turned off the tap, and listened to the cabin settle into night. The world beyond the windows widened into black. Somewhere in that dark a road led south; somewhere miles away a mortuary drawer had been shut. Somewhere a man practised a smirk. Here, a woman who had stopped speaking on the page laid her hand on the table and felt the old pulse answer: *You are still here, even if the story can't be.*

Exile was not a country but a season. It might hold. It might break. For now, the pines stood like tall, patient witnesses. The stove ticked its small metronome. And in the narrow bright of their clearing, silence went on doing the work it knows—keeping, carrying, covering—until morning asked for their names again.

Part V
They All Said Nothing

The Papers in the Dust

The summons came not as thunder but as a quiet envelope—cream-coloured, bureaucratic, addressed in block capitals to Cassandra's new post office box in Radium. The letterhead belonged to Carbon County's Office of Estates. Inside: a notice that the State had officially emptied the Whitaker house. Abby's possessions, it read in spare prose, had been inventoried, boxed, and archived. What mattered would be held; what did not would be discarded.

Cassandra held the paper in her hands as though it were a bone. The girls looked up from their card game at the kitchen table, eyes flickering to her face, then back down. Owen, at the stove, set down the spoon and came to her side. He read it silently, lips moving, then folded the page once, twice, slid it into his palm as if paper could bruise.

"Do you want me to call them?" he asked.

"No," Cassandra said. Her voice was steady, but something in her chest cracked as she spoke. "I'll go."

*   *   *   *   *

The house was no longer a house. It was a husk.

When Cassandra stepped through the door on a grey Pennsylvanian afternoon, the air met her like a blow. The smell of mildew and urine still lingered, but thinned now, overlaid by the antiseptic tang of strangers. Floors were stripped of rugs, wallpaper hung in curls, and dust gathered in a way that suggested no one had claimed the room as their own in years.

Boxes lined the hallway, each marked with numbers in black Sharpie. INVENTORY 14B. INVENTORY 27C. The language of reduction.

A clerk guided her through the rooms, reading off lists in a voice that had seen too much grief to soften anymore. Kitchen: chipped dishes, rusted tin, one cast-iron pan. Bedroom: a cedar chest, three faded quilts, unpaid bills dating back years. Living room: paperbacks swollen with damp, a sofa frame with stuffing clawed out.

And then: the drawer in Abby's room.

Inside were papers, loose, brittle, their edges greyed. Cassandra reached for them with the reverence one uses for old bones. There were bank slips from PNC—withdrawals made in the same hand, always in cash, always at odd intervals. There were copies of cheques signed with Abby's shaky scrawl and Darryl's neat countersignature beside it. There was the deed to the house, transferred.

And there was footage.

A small flash drive, labelled by a deputy. "Recovered from neighbour's camera, 2019." The clerk explained: the house across the lane had installed security cameras after a string of break-ins. One of them caught a fragment, filed away, nearly forgotten. Now unearthed.

Cassandra took it with hands that shook.

*   *   *   *   *

That night in the clerk's office, she watched.

The footage was grainy, black and white. The date stamp burned the corner: February, six years earlier. The lens caught the edge of Abby's porch, the dark silhouette of a man. Darryl. She knew the slope of those shoulders as she knew her own pulse.

He was shouting—though the camera captured no sound, the violence of it was written in his body, the way his hands slashed the air, the way his head thrust forward. Abby, small and frail in her housecoat, shook her head, held up her palms. She looked like someone begging weather to relent.

Then he struck.

Not a slap, not a push. A blow. The camera shuddered as though it felt it. Abby went down, crumpling against the railing, her body folding to the porch like something discarded. Darryl bent—not to help, but to seize her purse. He rifled through it, pocketed something, and left her there, small and broken against the steps, his image clear as he fled.

Cassandra's breath fractured in her chest.

The deputy fast-forwarded, neighbours shuffling quickly in and out of frame as they checked on Abby, still collapsed and unmoving. The stopped when the frame showed the ambulance lights flooding the porch twenty minutes later. Abby lifted onto stretcher, eyes glassy, lips moving with words no one would ever decode.

"That's when she stopped," Cassandra whispered. Her hands were cold, her throat raw. "That's when she... unravelled."

The deputy nodded grimly. "We never matched the assault report to this footage until now. It seems the neighbour supplied the footage to your mother and she, unsurprisingly, forgot about."

*   *   *   *

The paper trail told the rest.

Records of a remortgaged house, signed in a hand Abby could not have steadied. Statements showing her SSI cheques and Medicaid benefits siphoned into a joint account, then drained in cash withdrawals from casinos across three counties. Notes from collection agencies. Notices of foreclosure, barely held off by sporadic payments—sometimes by Cassandra herself, unknowingly filling a bucket that Darryl kept drilling holes into.

And the worst: dates after Abby's death. Benefits still collected, cheques still cashed, as though death itself were just another account to bleed.

Cassandra pressed her hands to her face, palms damp, as the deputy laid the evidence in order. Page after page, signature after signature. It was a cathedral of theft, built on her mother's failing mind, her failing body, her failing life.

*   *   *   *   *

When she returned to Radium, snow was falling. The girls met her at the door, their arms wrapping around her waist, their chatter anchoring her back to a world where breath still mattered. Owen carried her bag inside, then closed the door gently, as though sealing the mountains from whatever she had carried home.

That night, by low light, Cassandra spread the papers across the table. Owen read each one in silence, his mouth hardening, his hands tightening until the tendons showed like ropes. When he reached the footage still paused on her laptop, he turned away, shoulders stiff, throat working.

"After everything," Cassandra said, her voice breaking, "they'll see it. They'll finally see what he did."

Owen's hand found hers, fingers entwining. "And they'll see what you endured."

But Cassandra shook her head. She knew better. The world did not hunger for truth. It had already feasted on lies. What came next would not restore her. What came next would only weigh on Darryl.

Still—there was a bitter, aching satisfaction in knowing that at last, the proof existed. Proof carved into paper, burned into pixels, preserved in dust and drawer.

Her mother's ruin had not been madness, not accident. It had been a hand she knew too well.

And the hand was caught now, forever, in the eye of a machine that did not lie.

The Scales of Justice

The courtroom smelled of varnish and dust, the air heavy with the fatigue of centuries of verdicts. Cassandra sat in the second row, hands folded so tightly in her lap that her knuckles looked carved from bone. Owen was beside her, a steady weight at her side, but even his presence could not blunt the sharp edges of the moment.

It was not her case. It was the Commonwealth of Pennsylvania versus Darryl Whitaker and Wendy Kline. But the truth was threaded through her blood, and she felt every tick of the clock like a nerve pulled taut.

The district attorney spoke first. His voice was flat, clipped, not unkind but practical, like a man reciting coordinates. Theft by deception. Misuse of public benefits. Fraudulent remortgage. Continuing to collect after death. Assault resulting in permanent cognitive impairment. Each charge laid down like a stone, stacked until the weight became unbearable.

On the evidence screen: the footage.

The jurors flinched as Darryl's fist struck, as Abby folded to the porch, as his hand grabbed her purse. Cassandra closed her eyes, but she could still see it, etched into her skull. The courtroom was silent. When the lights brightened again, it felt obscene to breathe.

Then Darryl stood.

He was thicker now, age and wear showing at the seams, but the smirk still clung to him like mould. His lawyer leaned close, whispered, and Darryl nodded with theatrical reluctance. When he spoke, his voice was softer than she remembered, polished by coaching.

"I want to take responsibility," he said, hands clasped in front of him as if prayer could undo the stain. "I made mistakes. Gambling, drugs. I wasn't in my right mind. I love my mother. I didn't mean for any of this to happen. But I can't undo what I did. I can only say I'm sorry."

Cassandra felt bile rise. The words were rehearsed, hollow, the performance of contrition with no actions behind them. Yet the system sometimes made space for performance. Cassandra held her breath and waited.

The judge's gaze was heavy, his robes a shadow that seemed to gather the weight of the room. He spoke slowly, the way old men speak when they want each word to be a nail in a coffin.

"Mr. Whitaker, you stole from your own mother. You assaulted her in such a way that she never recovered. And then you continued to exploit her— even in death. This court has seen many kinds of theft, but few so cruel, few so intimate. Your actions hollowed out a life that should have been protected. They hollowed out your sister's faith in justice. They hollowed out the community's trust."

Darryl's eyes darted toward Cassandra then, quick and sharp, as if to remind her that even in defeat he could still aim his blade. She did not look away.

The gavel struck once. "You will serve no less than five years and no more than seven years in the State Correctional Institution. Restitution to the estate of your mother will be ordered, though it will never equal what was taken."

A murmur rippled through the gallery. Cassandra exhaled, long and shaky, her body trembling as though the words themselves had weight.

Then Wendy's turn came.

She looked smaller than Cassandra remembered—her blouse buttoned to the throat, hair pulled tight as though order could substitute for innocence. Her lawyer painted her as an accessory, a woman swept along in the wake of Darryl's addictions. "She did not strike. She did not scheme. She looked away. And for that, she is guilty. But she is also capable of reform."

The judge listened, his face carved from stone.

"Ms. Kline," he said at last, "you stood beside a man who drained the life from his mother and his sister. You did not stop him. You benefited from his crimes. The law recognises complicity, but it also recognises capacity for change. You will receive a suspended sentence of two years with probation. You will perform community service and attend financial counselling. But know this—silence, when it enables harm, is not neutral. It is betrayal."

Wendy nodded quickly, eyes downcast, but Cassandra caught the flicker of relief in her shoulders, the way she already seemed to be calculating her next step.

The gavel fell again.

It was finished.

Outside, the courthouse steps glared in the autumn sun. The reporters who had once swarmed around this case were absent now. Justice, unlike scandal, rarely made good copy. The air smelled faintly of leaves and exhaust, and the town moved around them as though nothing had shifted.

But inside Cassandra, something had.

Not victory. The sentence would not restore her career, or cleanse the ridicule, or erase the chants of burn the bitch. It would not give her or her family back their lives, or the girl who had once believed truth alone could save her.

But it was weight, at last, on the other side of the scale. Not enough, never enough. Yet something.

Owen touched her hand, threading their fingers together as they descended the steps. His warmth steadied her.

"They'll be locked away," he murmured.

"For a while. At least he will be" she said.

"And Wendy?"

Cassandra looked out across the valley, the ridges rising like walls, the sky stretched thin and cold. "She'll keep living with what she did. Sometimes that's the harsher sentence."

The wind lifted, carrying the courthouse flag into a hard snap. Cassandra closed her eyes against the sting. For the first time in years, she felt the faintest tilt in the compass within her. Not triumph, not healing, but the smallest suggestion of balance.

The scales had shifted.

And for now, that was enough.

The Mourning

They drove home the way people leave cemeteries—slowly, without announcing it to the road. The highway slid under them like a dark ribbon; the mountains gathered dusk in their folds and held it. It was September in the Columbia Valley, a thin edge of cold already sharpening the evenings. When they turned down the rutted track toward the clearing, the lodgepole pines closed around them like a privacy they had earned with silence.

The cabin lights came on in stages—porch first, then the kitchen, then the small lamp by the bookshelf that made its own little lake of gold. Maggie had left a stew warming in the crock and a note on the counter in a tidy hand: Girls finished their homework. Fire banked. Call if you need anything; otherwise, I will see myself out. Love you all. Beneath it, two apples sat in a bowl with a sprig of late mint, as if the province itself had arranged a small still life to recognize the day's ending.

Eve and Eden barreled down the ladder from the loft the moment the truck door slammed. The hug hurt, which was how Cassandra knew she'd been bracing her ribs against the world all day. The twins spoke on top of each other, a braid of questions and reassurances—Did it happen? Are you hungry? Do you need us to set the table?—and then, catching something in their mother's face, they quieted in that instinctive way children have when love is doing arithmetic in a room.

They ate at the pine table with the window cracked and the night leaning in. No one said *court* or *sentence*. They spoke instead of the creek being low, a woodpecker drilling the shed, an elk cow spotted at the treeline with a calf the colour of tea. The stew was spare and honest, carrots sweet as if they had decided not to argue with the pot. Owen buttered bread with the attention of a man making a promise he could keep. Cassandra found herself counting the beads of condensation on her water glass, the shape of her girls' hands as they broke their bread, the soft thud of their heels against chair rungs—proofs of life she understood better than verdicts.

After dinner, Eden did the washing up—she liked the system of it—while Eve dried and performed a monologue about a moth that had mistaken their porch light for a second moon. They carried the warm plates up the ladder and tucked themselves into the loft with their paperbacks, backs propped against the rail. Owen checked the stove, set a fresh log, and ran a practised palm along the seam of the door to feel for stray heat. The cabin exhaled and settled; the valley listened.

When the girls were asleep, Owen took down two glasses from the shelf, the good ones with the small nick at the base from the move, and poured a white wine that smelled of stone and peach. He carried them to the table and waited, because he had learned that bringing a thing to Cassandra was different than asking her to come to it. She sat, and her chair creaked its familiar note.

To drink was to admit the day was over. She did not want it to be over—not because it had been good (it had not), but because endings declared themselves and she had stopped trusting declarations. Still, she lifted the glass and tasted, and a warmth opened in her chest that was not relief and not joy but something like a truce.

They spoke around the wound first. He asked about the drive. She told him the light had a copper to it, as if the mountains were bruised with evening. He told her about a recent day the pump had sulked and then cooperated, that the girls had argued about who would refill the kindling basket and then done it together, and that Maggie had described the stew as "parsimonious in the best sense," which made him laugh. She told him the courthouse had smelled of varnish and dust and old air. He nodded his agreement, travelling back to the courthouse all those days away now.

When the second glass was half gone, the careful architecture of the weeks of travel and the trial gave way. Cassandra placed her forearms on the table as if setting down something heavy, and the tears came without preamble. They were not wrenching sobs at first. They were clean and inexorable, the body's answer to too much carrying.

Owen stood and came around the table. He didn't pull her up or fold over her. He knelt beside her, close enough that their shoulders touched, and set his hand on the back of her neck in that way he had learned when the ground pitched. She cried into the curve of her elbow, the kind of crying that makes no sound until you hear the breath break.

"They believed me," she said finally, the words blurred, soft. "Or—no. That's not it. The court believed the papers. The footage. The sequence of events. Not me. I'm not sure anyone ever believed me—just the proof. And even that came too late to save what it needed to save."

He didn't argue. The wine smelled suddenly of metal and sunlight. Outside, the night had deepened into true dark; the ridge was a single shape, a held breath.

"I wanted it to feel like something," she said. "Not triumph. Just... balance. A weight set down. But it doesn't. It feels like an entry in a ledger after the doors have closed and the lights are off. It feels like mathematics after a funeral."

"That's what justice looks like most days," Owen said gently. "Bookkeeping." He tilted his head. "But sometimes bookkeeping keeps the roof from caving in."

She let out a sound that might have been a laugh before it broke. "I am so tired," she whispered. "Of telling the truth to rooms that prefer stories."

He pressed his lips to the crown of her head. "Then don't tell them," he said. "Tell me. Tell the girls. Tell the trees if you like. Or tell no one for a while and let your body believe itself again."

She turned her face toward him then, and the weeping sharpened, unlocked from its discipline. It took her apart. She made the small animal sounds people make when the container of grief fails. He held. No speeches, no counsel. Just the human fact of him alight against the fact of her undoing. The stove ticked; a knot popped in the log; the cabin gathered them closer with its wooden lungs.

When tears finally burned down to salt and breath, he wiped her cheeks with his thumbs and refilled their glasses in the quiet way of a man setting the evening back on its rails.

"I want to go to the press," he said—the words soft, not an argument so much as an offering laid on the table. "Not tabloids or anyone who sold you out—real reporters. We can share the filings, the footage. We can ask them to print the whole of it. Your name deserves the truth as loudly as the lie."

Cassandra stilled. She looked at his face—its open wanting, which was not vanity, not machismo, but a husband's old fury encountering a fresh door.

She lifted her glass, set it down, then placed her hand over his on the table so he would know the refusal was not a rejection of him.

"I can't," she said. "Not because they don't deserve it. Because I do. I deserve to stop being a headline. I deserve to stop dragging my story behind me like tin cans tied to a bumper. I want to make quiet the place where my name lives."

He winced, but he understood. She felt him understand, the micro-relaxation through his fingers, the slow exhale that conceded ground and made camp on what remained. He turned his palm under hers and threaded their fingers so that refusal became a kind of binding.

"Okay," he said. "Then I won't."

"Thank you," she whispered.

They sat like that long enough for the wine to warm in the glass and the night to lift an owl from the treeline to the air. Upstairs, a body slid against a mattress and then stilled. The girls re-entered their dreams. The stove sighed. Cassandra breathed the smell of resin and smoke and something faintly floral she couldn't place—maybe the mint Maggie had left in the bowl, a small grace travelling.

The next morning, Radium woke to a thin frost on the grass that burned off by ten. Owen drove down to the post office on his Thursday circuit. In the box, among a coupon flyer and a hand-addressed envelope from Maggie, was a copy of the Columbia Valley Pioneer. On the bottom half of the front page, beneath a photograph of a new bear-proof bin being installed at the school, a headline in sensible type read:

Pennsylvania Man Sentenced in Elder Fraud; Assault Footage Cited

The article was six paragraphs. It named the man, the charges, the sentence; it mentioned a sister who had filed early complaints and been maligned; it noted that proof had later substantiated the pattern. It did not print Cassandra's pen name. It did not refer to the scandal, the hashtags, the chants. It ended with a line about the obligation of systems to protect the vulnerable.

Owen brought it home, laid it next to the kettle while the girls cut sandwiches into triangles, and waited for Cassandra to come in from the woodpile. She washed her hands, saw the paper, and read it standing. Her mouth made a shape like relief, though nothing rushed in to fill it.

"Will it help?" he asked, and he already knew the answer, but asking is a form of respect.

"It helps that it exists," she said. "It helps that someone bothered to write it down as if it were ordinary and required no spectacle."

They checked the paper's website later, almost by accident. The story had three comments. One was a neighbour in Invermere saying, Good to see justice somewhere. One was a man complaining about the misuse of tax dollars. One was spam. The post gathered no heat, no swarm, no echo. By afternoon, it was buried under a piece about a farmers' market vendor retiring her jam spoon.

No calls came. No apologies. No reversals from publishers. No editors knocking politely on an inbox. The valley kept the weather it had. The creek moved as it always did along the rocks that never asked to be thanked.

That night, they ate roasted potatoes and eggs, because somehow the simplest meals are the ones that account for grief without comment. After the girls were asleep, Cassandra and Owen carried their glasses to the porch and sat with their ankles touching, facing the dark. The ridge was a single shoulder. Somewhere a truck took the highway's curve with a faith she envied. Wind moved through the pines in a sound like low water over stones.

"Tell me something true," Owen said quietly, not as a test, but as a way to invite the night to do its work.

Cassandra thought for a long time. Then: "We did the right thing," she said. "And it didn't save us. And I would do it again."

He nodded, and in his nod she heard me too. A moth knocked gently at the porch light and then reconsidered.

She finished her wine and set the empty glass beside her foot. The cool rose up off the ground, the kind of cold that says *winter is waiting at the edge of the yard.* She threaded her fingers with his again and closed her eyes, and for once the darkness did not feel like a mouth; it felt like a room with no corners.

The bear bin clanged somewhere over by the school. A late bird tried out a note and then took it back. The cabin listened in both directions—to the ridge, to the people on the porch—and held what it could.

A breeze lifted and let go. A dog barked twice and fell silent. In the clearing, nothing dramatic came, no fanfare on behalf of the correct. The world made the same sounds it had made yesterday and would make tomorrow.

The truth came out, and all it was, was quiet.

You've Reached The End But...
The Stories Never Stop

Songs To Stories is exactly what it sounds like—short, emotionally devastating, romantically charged, and occasionally unhinged novellas inspired by the one and only Taylor Swift. Because why simply listen to a song when you can spiral into an entire fictional universe about it?

A new novella drops on the 13th and 21st of every month, so if you have commitment issues, don't worry—you don't have to wait long for your next dose of heartbreak, longing, and characters making wildly questionable life choices in the name of love.

To keep up with the latest releases, visit <u>BrittWolfe.com</u>—or don't, and risk missing out while the rest of us are already crying over the next one. Your call.

See you at the next emotional wreckage.

About The Author

Britt Wolfe

Britt Wolfe was born in Fort McMurray, Alberta, and now lives in Calgary, where she battles snow, writes stories, and cries over Taylor Swift lyrics like the proud elder Swiftie she is. She loves being part of a fan base that's as passionate as it is melodramatic.

She's married to a smoking hot Australian (her words, but also probably everyone else's), and together they parent two fur-babies: Sophie, the most perfect husky in the universe, and Lena, a mischievous cat who keeps them on their toes—and their furniture in shreds.

When Britt's not writing or re-listening to "All Too Well (10 Minute Version)," she's indulging her love for reading, potatoes in all forms, and the colour green. She's also a huge fan of polar bears, tigers, red pandas, otters, Nile crocodiles, and—because they're underrated—donkeys.

Her life is full of love, laughter, and just enough chaos to keep things interesting.

 @the.banality.of.britt

 BrittWolfe.com